A Scout's Salute

Authors Choice Press

San Jose New York Lincoln Shanghai

A Scout's Salute

Authors Choice Press
an imprint of iUniverse.com, Inc.

For information address:
iUniverse.com, Inc.
5220 S 16th, Ste. 200
Lincoln, NE 68512
www.iuniverse.com

Originally published by Vantage Press, Inc

ISBN: 0-595-18167-8

Printed in the United States of America

To all who have worn a scout uniform with pride—
especially those who have seen the arrow

Contents

A Scout's Salute

Gary

It was time for breakfast and Gary couldn't find his frying pan. He knew it had to be somewhere nearby because he had used it for supper the previous night. He checked the patrol box, but it wasn't there. Neither was it by his tent. At least he couldn't see it there. But too many clothes and too much camping equipment were scattered around for him to make a thorough search. His hunger pangs were making Gary's search increasingly frantic. Gary was a six-meal-a-day scout. Without a good breakfast, he couldn't possibly focus his efforts properly on preparing his mid-morning snack.

As he threw a couple of more logs on the smoldering fire, Gary spied the handle of the skillet nearly lost among the needles of the pine branches of the firewood pile. With a dexterity that belied his rotund form, Gary snatched the frying pan, waved a few of the twigs and some of the dirt off that had collected on the congealed hamburger drippings left in the pan from a previous meal. He dropped it with a thud on the grill that perched precariously over the fire, seeming at any moment about to collapse in a heap of scrap metal.

Waiting until the grease had melted, but before it started to smoke, Gary dropped in thick slices of the potatoes that he had found under the wood pile when he found his skillet. The grime on his hands from two days of camping had, to that point, resisted all of his efforts to remove it by repeatedly wiping his hands on his scout pants. Moisture from the potatoes dissolved a few of the layers from his hands and coated the potato slices, giving them a uniform sludge-gray appearance.

Before the potatoes could begin to steam, Gary cracked

1

into the skillet the three eggs that had managed to stay intact in the carton. The odd pieces of eggshell that dropped in with the potatoes added a stark contrast to the potatoes. He remembered that Max Bauer, his scoutmaster, had told him that to taste best, camp food should be pleasing to the eye. The use of contrasting colors was one way to make food appealing. Gary was delighted with the white on black/gray appearance of his food as he contemplated his early morning creation. He was so impressed that he decided to share it with Max. "Boy, won't he be surprised when I take breakfast to him. He is still asleep and sunrise will be in a half-hour."

Thinking that the eggshell white was a great idea, Gary added six torn-up slices of bread for a little body, and stirred the concoction so that it wouldn't stick to the pan. He was overwhelmed by the magnificence of his creation and the brilliance of his idea to surprise Max. "He will be so amazed at my culinary skills, that maybe he will let me be a patrol leader."

As the mixture began to steam, but long before it would have bubbled, Gary pronounced it finished, probably his finest camp creation yet, a mere hint of entrées to come.

Knocking off some of the larger pieces of crud stuck to an old tin plate he found lying around, Gary searched for some eating utensils but could only find a partially buried fork, which he picked up, popped in his mouth, sucked on for a moment, and then wiped on the seat of his pants. *It will do,* he thought as he scooped some of the contents of the frying pan onto the tin plate.

The sun was just peeking over a forested hill as Gary proudly marched toward his scoutmaster's tent with breakfast. Gary paused for a moment to ponder the beauty in the solitude of the sunrise. The dew sparkled on a thousand blades of grass. Red-winged blackbirds called stridently near the lake shore. In the distance a loon welcomed the new day with her madman's laugh. The waves lapped the shore, hurried along by a morning breeze. Near an overhanging tree, a trout leaped into the air, intent on a hovering nymph, and becoming a momentary fair-weather rainbow hanging in a cloudless sky, before splashing delicately back to the crystalline waters. Across the small lake, a beaver set out for a morning snack of poplar shoots, her wake leaving a placid V-shape behind her, emphatically marking the passage of the magnificent swimmer. Clouds near the tree tops were painted in pastels of a giant's creative palette. Gary was glad he was a scout, thankful for the opportunity to camp and hike with other boys.

Max's tent was nearly hidden in a cedar thicket. Max was his hero. Max was an Eagle scout, something Gary wanted to be someday. He was also in the Order of the Arrow. As a twelve-year-old boy, Gary had carefully watched Max on several camp-outs. He noticed that Max's tent was always clean and ship-shape. Gary couldn't remember a time when Max's uniform wasn't clean and neatly pressed. His boots were always laced up, looking worn but comfortable. Max's red wool scout jacket was spotless and stood out against the green of the forest like a British soldier's. The brim on his campaign hat was stiff as if starched daily. When he dined, even on a campout, Max always kept a clean kitchen and his food looked appetizing. At night his lantern always cast a cheery net over the boys in the troop, welcoming them to sit around his campfire, sing old scouting songs, and listen to tales of what scouting was like when Max was a boy before the war.

Max was always teaching boys about life. He was never too busy to talk about problems boys had. He had a pretty wife who cared about boys just as much as Max did. If Max wasn't at home, she always welcomed boys in and listened as if she had nothing more important to do than be a scout's second mom. She was a gem of a person: sparkling, brilliant, priceless. She was Max's Lillian, his Diamond Lil. Gary had decided that he wanted to be like Max someday.

He was in the process of doing that now. Shaking off the trance of sunrise, Gary continued towards Max's tent but didn't see the root sticking up even after it tripped him. As he fell into a cedar tree, Gary could smell the freshness of the flat, palmated cedar needles. It reminded him of the time Max had taken him trout fishing. After catching his very first fish, an

3

eight-inch-long rainbow trout, and proudly showing it to Max, he had not known what to do with the fish. He wanted to take it home to eat, but was afraid it would dry out before he got there. Max had showed him how to break off a couple of small cedar branches, dip them in the stream, and then wrap them around the fish. The moisture on the branches would keep the fish damp. Since then, Gary had fished a few more times and kept his fish fresh with wet cedar branches. For Gary, the smell of cedar always brought back the pleasant memories of fishing in the cool woods on a warm summer day.

Now the smell of cedar was the odor of disaster. The old tin plate slipped from his fingers and, as he fell helplessly entangled in cedar branches, dealt him a glancing blow on the head before falling in slow motion to land on some branches a split-second after Gary stopped falling to lie gracelessly on a cedar throne. Since the broken eggs were only lukewarm, they dripped off his scout hat, making momentary stalactites that sparkled in the morning sun. Potato disks were everywhere and bread hunks were already attracting a blue jay who sat in a nearby tree, shouting breakfast news to other jays nearby. As Gary looked up, he found himself gazing into Max's merry eyes. In the early morning light, they seemed to have an added twinkle.

"I was bringing you breakfast, Max," whimpered Gary. "It was really good. I'm sorry, Max. I seem to have spilled it," he continued, looking mournfully around the chaos he had created.

He spotted the tin plate, lying upright on a couple of branches with a few pieces of potato clinging desperately to it. Some bread hunks were on his lap. *It's not too dirty*, Gary thought as he surveyed the wreckage. *I can still salvage something from this.*

As the smile of a solution flashed across Gary's face, Max recognized it and quickly said, "Thanks, Gary. I appreciate your efforts. Let's get this cleaned up and we'll make some breakfast together."

4

Pierre

Pierre was the oldest boy in the troop, being a few years older than most of the other scouts. He had been a scout for five years and, in that time, had become a Star scout. He was a husky scout with curly hair, freckles, and a winning smile. He owned a bugle from which he could coax a pitifully small number of notes, each of them brash and usually having no melodic relationship to the one immediately before or after it. He wore a campaign hat with the front and back brims bent up so that it looked like a vulute spreading its wings so the sunlight would kill any remaining bacteria following dinner on a dead delicacy. A rumor circulated in the troop that Pierre had been known to invite scouts who failed to live up to his high expectations of scout behavior to a secluded copse of trees and informally counseling them on the error of their ways. According to the rumor, said scouts, having been dutifully counseled, recognized the error of their ways and got their scouting act together. Once, when asked about the truthfulness of the rumors concerning Pierre, Max responded, with a straight face, that he knew nothing about it. We believed him, of course.

Pierre was our senior patrol leader. He could light a fire with one match, lash any number of poles together, perform adequate first aid on any injury imaginable, and read the story told by tracks in the dirt or snow. Pierre could tie most knots with his eyes closed, could move a canoe faster with his hands than most scouts could with a paddle, and cook food that was, if not delicious, at least recognizable. He had his own cup that he kept in Max's tent, from which he drank steaming campfire coffee with Max as we sat around the fire. He could climb trees, fly kites, and hike prodigious distances. Unfortunately, once out of sight of the camp, he had absolutely no idea where he was or how to return to where he had been. Worse, he seldom recognized that he was lost, even in the face of overwhelming evidence. It was wise to send someone on a hike with Pierre who knew his way around the woods.

After dinner on the day of Gary's breakfast fiasco, Pierre decided that the troop needed to take a leisurely stroll to look at plants and observe the forest animals as evening approached. Gathering the fifteen boys together, like a mother hen assembling her brood, Pierre told Max that they would head out through the woods to the main highway, turn right, and return to camp by another trail through the woods. "Okay," said Max. "Try to be back by dark."

"No problem," said Pierre, and led the troop off to look at Lady's Slippers, mushrooms, and Lilies of the Valley. The northern woods, in the spring, is a peaceful place to be. A splash of red signaled a cardinal flashing from tree to bush. Nut hatches and woodpeckers skittered up and down tree trunks, looking for hidden insects on which to dine. The raucous cries of the blue jays were delicious to the ear. Fat pine grosbeaks with their chisel jaws were a yellow counterpoint with their evening songs. In the distance the haunting cry of the whippoorwill and the lonely call of a mourning dove made a duet of sadness in the evening stillness. Squirrels chittered in the trees, as scouts hiked past, thinking what a strange lot they were. The odd porcupine waddled across the trail seeking a solitary dinner of succulent tree bark.

The wind, screaming through the wings of a night hawk as she fell through the sky dining on flying insects, made them close the gaps in the line of scouts, the noise being both intimate and intimidating. The flash of white on the tail of a deer seen for mere seconds before disappearing in the woods was something rarely viewed by a troop of scouts. Pierre showed all nature's wonders to the scouts. Around the lakes, the trails left by beavers as they dragged their winter's supply of limbs and branches to their underwater pantry, led to the water's edge. Tracks of beaver, raccoon, and muskrat were recorded in the chronicles of mud along the water's edge. The heart-stopping crash of a partridge as it flushed from under their feet brought on sudden laughter to cover up the scouts' momentary fright. A woodcock rose like a feathered helicopter and startled the scouts before rocketing through the trees, dodging and twisting to miss the branches in its rush from danger, not nearly matching the boys' fright or the wonder they felt as Pierre pointed out the path of the fleeing, feathered terror.

They heard the ubiquitous loon's call answered, from farther out in the lake, by a lifetime mate, the loons sharing sonnets of love as they floated serenely in the deepening shadows of the shimmering waters. The loon's mystical, magical, maniacal melody sent shivers up and down their spines like the tiny footsteps of a thousand ants marching in unison.

As dusk turned slowly to darkness, John, the Eagle patrol leader, had his first inkling that they were, indeed, on another Pierre hike. They reached the highway and were blinded by the light of a passing car. The light must have fogged Pierre's mind because he turned left instead of right as he had told Max he would.

"Wrong turn, Pierre," John offered as he began the laborious process of convincing Pierre that he knew where they were and Pierre didn't.

"Naw!" Pierre said. "The trail we need is just ahead," he responded with his usual confidence. "We'll be back in no time."

"Hokay," John muttered to him. "I wonder how worried Max will be when we don't show up when we should."

They followed the road for about a mile when they came to an intersection of highways.

"Pierre, if we go back now, we can find the path we followed from camp and be back in time for hot chocolate around the campfire," John pleaded, trying hard not to sound like that was what he was doing.

"We need to turn left here and we will find a trail that returns to camp," insisted Pierre.

"No it won't," John volunteered. "I hiked this route five

times last summer when I earned a hiking merit badge. It will get us back to camp all right but just in time for breakfast."

"We turn left," Pierre said, leading the scouts down the left side of the road and launching into an off key version of *I'm Happy When I'm Hiking*. The scouts reluctantly joined him in singing only as a defense to drown out Pierre's music, which, like his route-finding, was awful.

It was too dark to see anything. The scouts were on a road deep in the woods with no nearby lakes. No cars broke the monotony and only the distant plea of a whippoorwill and the spooky hooting of an owl kept them company as they each silently vowed to never take another hike with Pierre.

By midnight, Pierre accepted the inevitable. He was lost, had no idea how to return to face the music with Max, and had a crew of thoroughly tired boy scouts with him. Even though his legs screamed with fatigue, John tried to encourage the others by standing while they rested, patting them on the back to show appreciation for what they had done up to that point, and telling them that they could do it. John assured them that they would be back in camp by breakfast. They were a miserable, tired, hungry bunch of campers.

They reached a point where a power line cut through the forest, passing between two uninhabited lakes and intersecting the highway the scouts had come upon when first leaving the woods but about four miles west of camp. It was a long mile following the power poles, but even Pierre could not lose them in the dark. The scouts stumbled along the cleared path of the power line, now lit from above by a quarter moon and a blanket of stars. Pierre tried to teach them about the movement of the stars in the heavens as they shuffled along, but no one seemed to notice. They were more interested in finding a rope and a convenient tree to test the weight-bearing capacity of various scout knots. Pierre seemed oblivious to the undercurrent of feeling flowing toward him. None of the scouts would join in singing trail songs. No one would tell a story. Everyone had withdrawn into himself as he dragged one foot in front of another.

They reached the highway at two in the morning. The scouts could go no farther. They collapsed in a heap, sprawling over each other, seeking a comfortable resting place to spend their last few minutes of life since they knew they were going to die. John volunteered to flag down a car, if one happened to come by, catch a ride to the trail they had used earlier, and hike back to camp to get Max. Miraculously, a car appeared. In those days it was still safe to stop and help someone stranded along a highway in the middle of the night. The hero who stopped gladly offered John a ride down the road.

John stumbled into camp near 4:00 A.M. Max was sitting by his campfire, composing his letter of resignation just before committing hari-kari. Startled by John's footsteps because he heard the approach of the lone scout rather than the whole troop, Max's face showed relief when John assured him the troop members were still alive but a little tired. Max and John hopped in his red-and-white station wagon and came close to setting the land-speed record for travel on a dirt road through a forest in the dark. Max told John along the way that he had made a big pot of hot chocolate for the boys at dark when he thought they would be returning. It had long since turned as cold as the reception John expected from Max.

They had a hard time awakening the boys even with the bright lights of the car glaring in their eyes. Stacking the scouts in the car was not unlike scattering firewood around. It didn't matter the order just so the boys all fit in the car.

"You guys sure had me worried," was all that Max said on the subject that morning.

Back at camp, Max helped dump scouts in their sleeping bags and returned to his vigil by the fire. Pierre and John sheepishly tried to join him, but Max waved them off. With their tails between their legs, Pierre and John slunk into their bags and fell into a dreamless sleep.

By nine o'clock all of the scouts were up and about. Everyone was cheerful. No one commented negatively on Gary's gastronomic delights even if they wouldn't eat any of what he so willingly shared. No one wanted to hang Pierre. Max brought

9

the troop members together around the camp fire.

"What did you learn?" Max inquired.

The scouts talked about how hard the hike was, how easy it was to get discouraged, and how much their feet hurt. Then they talked about the beauty of the night, all of the sounds they had remembered, how chilling the sounds were at night, but not scary at all now as they talked about them in the daylight. They talked about how they had come to depend on each other. The scouts agreed that the experience would have been unbearable alone, but with good friends, it was not so daunting. It was fortunate that one's body forgets pain. Or maybe, from pain, the body forges the steel of learning. In any event, the scouts looked back on the previous evening's experience with awe and wonder. They were amazed at what they had accomplished, so much that was beyond their imagination the previous morning. They also wondered why they had been suckered into another Pierre hike.

But that hike added to the legend of Pierre. It became a matter of honor that a scout had hiked with Pierre. The more hikes successfully survived, the higher the scout's status. Rather than berate them for wandering around in the dark all night, Max let his scouts use the experience to teach them things about themselves and about courage and endurance that would help them all later in life.

Spring Camporee

It had been late when the flashlights were finally turned off for the night. Steve was tired as he wearily crawled in his sleeping bag. Etched in his mind was the memory of the buglers, silhouetted against the pink-tinged clouds, their bugles pressed to their lips, facing each other near the flag pole at the crest of the hill. The haunting notes of *Taps* from the first bugler were softly repeated by the second, the notes echoing across the camp, a gentle reminder for scouts to end the day with reverent silence. It was his first council-wide activity, and Steve was excited to be camping with two thousand other scouts. Troops from all over the northern part of the state were camped on the hillside, their campfires and lanterns twinkling in the night, their laughter and songs drifting on a gentle evening breeze. Wood smoke wafted across the grassy slopes, an aromatic airborne magnet that enticed the nose with a smorgasbord of smells. Around the margins of the camp, fireflies glided in the evening sky, like dim mobile lighthouses, dancing to an inner melody orchestrated by Nature.

As was the custom, Max had picked up the scouts at the centrally located, old Elmwood school at 5:30 P.M. His old reliable milk truck was stuffed with scouts and their camping gear. Scouts sat on patrol boxes, packs, tent sacks, and duffel bags for the fifty-mile journey to the hillside park where the council was holding a spring camporee. In the weeks prior to departure, Max had his scouts review scouting skills that they would use in inter-troop competition: fire starting, making knots, compass-reading, lashing, cooking, first aid, and scout spirit.

Arriving later than he had wanted to, Max had registered his troop and found their assigned camping area near the bottom of the rolling hill. Pierre, his senior patrol leader, had assigned patrols to their camping areas and had supervised the construction of Troop 35's tent city. After a quick dinner, Max gathered his scouts around the campfire for some last-minute encouragement and songs. Penultimately, as was the tradition in the troop, Max offered the scouts an opportunity to share any feelings that needed to be expressed prior to retiring for the night. He had found that scouts most often wanted to express gratitude to each other for helping out when no help was expected. Occasionally, feelings had been hurt or feathers ruffled. Max found it helpful to have those feelings out in the open lest they fester through the night, providing the fuel for a morning fight.

Finally, Max offered the *Scoutmaster's Minute.* "I'm really proud of you guys," he said. "The patrol leaders have done a great job teaching skills to their scouts. We have a good-looking camp. Pierre, you have done your usual good job of getting the camp set up quickly and correctly. Our new tents look great. We have the best-looking camp and the best scouts in the council. Thanks, you guys. See you in the morning."

Steve, Mark, and Roger shared a tent. They were in the Eagle patrol. All of them were working on the requirements for Tenderfoot. As they zipped up their tent for the night, Steve exulted, "Wow! Can you believe we are here at last? I didn't think this weekend would ever get here. Isn't scouting great?"

Steve woke up as the robins began to sing in the nearby trees. It was still dark out as he stretched in his sleeping bag, willing the sun to speed up its journey so he could more quickly dress in his new scout uniform and neckerchief. Steve drifted back to sleep, dreaming about camping, hiking, and canoe trips.

When reveille sounded at 6:30, Steve realized that in the short time since he had listened to the robins, a light mist had fallen. *The new tents must leak,* he thought, tucking in his shirt. His new red neckerchief was now purple. *Somehow it got wet,* he continued his conversation to himself. "Hey, Mark. Get up. Everything's wet in here."

Groggily, Mark raised up on his elbows to survey the contents of the tent.

"Hey, my neckerchief is purple," grunted Mark, as he elbowed the still-supine Roger. "Roger, get up. Something weird is going on."

"What?" mumbled Roger, eyes bleary as they tried to focus on the new day. Then sitting bolt upright on the floor of the tent, he asked, "Steve, have you been eating raspberries? Your lips are purple."

Steve reached for his mouth, running his hands across his lips and examining his fingers in the dim light of the tent.

"No," he responded. "Your lips are purple, too."

Fumbling with the tent zipper, Steve was finally able to free himself from the confines of his cotton cocoon. He dashed over to his scoutmaster's tent, shouting as he went, "Max! Help, Max!"

"Calm down, Steve. What seems to be the problem?" questioned Max, who was sitting in his rocking chair, savoring a cup of early morning coffee before his scouts arose.

"My lips are purple. And my neckerchief," he said, holding it out in offering. "What should I do? Am I sick? Am I going to die?"

"Well, now, let me see," said Max. "Maybe I'm seeing things, but this neckerchief looks red to me. And your lips don't seem to be purple any more." A twinkle danced around Max's eyes as a smile highlighted his big, square teeth. "You set up your tent late last night, didn't you? And you didn't get in it until after dark?"

Gnawing on his lower lip, Steve tried to remember the sequence of events during the rush to set up camp. "That's right, Max."

"Go back into your tent, see what happens, then come back and tell me what you saw," suggested Max. "I'll wait here for your report."

Sheepishly, Steve returned to Max. "It turned purple in

the tent and red when I came back out," he said, indicating the neckerchief in his hand. "The same with my lips. But why?"

"Why do you think it happened, Steve?" asked Max, gently.

Steve began to worry his lower lip again, kicking at the ground with the tips of his boots. Everything had looked wet in the tent, but when he touched things, they were actually dry. He assumed they were wet because everything that was supposed to be red had turned purple. Then he thought about the new tents and their light green cotton material.

"It's the green fabric of the tent," said Steve, snapping up his head to look at Max. "It makes red things look purple."

"You got it, ace," congratulated Max. "Now go get your patrol leader up. We've got a lot to do today."

After breakfast, the Eagle patrol members left their campsite to begin the competition with the rest of the troops. At the compass-reading activity, Steve had to take a bearing on a stake pounded into the ground about a hundred feet away. He pointed the stationary arrow of the plastic compass platform at the stake and slowly turned the dial on the compass until the moving arrow inside the dial lined up with the arrow painted on the floor of the dial. Then he put a brown grocery sack over his head, obstructing his forward view. Holding the compass close to his chest, he had to keep the arrow in the dial lined up while he slowly walked in the direction indicated by the third arrow. Steve resisted the temptation to peek out from under the edge of the sack, and as a reward for his honesty, five minutes later, he stumbled over the implanted stake. The other scouts in the Eagle patrol were equally successful.

At the knot area, two poles were placed in the ground about four feet apart. Joining them together about twenty feet in the air, was a six-foot pole, lashed perpendicularly to the poles. It looked to Steve like the big swing set his dad had built at home but without the rope and board seat. Beyond the vertical poles was a three-foot pine log. On the near side, but twenty feet from it, was a stake driven into the ground and angled away from the vertical poles. There were two such

14

structures, side-by-side. A designated scout from each patrol had to pick up a length of rope, coil it efficiently, and throw it over the horizontal log attached to the poles. Dropping the rope, the scout had to race forwards, pick up the hanging end, and tie a timber hitch to the three-foot log before running back to the coil of rope he had left on the ground. Grabbing the rope, the scout needed to pull the log into the air and secure the rope end to the stake in the ground using a clove hitch. To provide extra incentive, scouts from two patrols ran the event simultaneously. Steve was proud when all of the scouts in his patrol successfully completed the knot activity.

As the Eagles travelled from activity to activity, they practiced their patrol yells and scout songs. Each carried a hiking stick for support. As they approached a log that crossed a creek ambling across the lower portion of the camping area, a patrol from another troop was heading for the same log but going in the opposite direction. They, too, were carrying walking sticks. Dave, patrol leader of the Eagles, reached the near end of the log just as the other patrol arrived at the far side. Both patrol leaders edged out on the log, measuring the weight of the other and the size of the opponent's walking stick. At the center, modern-day Robin Hood met Little John. With a sudden slash, the other patrol leader brought his hiking stick into play. Dave was able to block the thrust, but in doing so lost his balance. Desperately he tried to remain upright, but a nudge from his opponent cartwheeled him into the pool under the log.

Struggling to the surface, Dave grinned while sputtering, "Get him, guys." And the contest was joined. Wood thunked against wood as the remaining scouts closed in a mock battle. Scouts toppled off the log like trees being felled in a tornado, laughing as they fell, entangled in each other's arms and legs. When the brief encounter was finished, no one was left on the log, but everyone emerged a winner. Noting the troop number and town on each other's uniforms, both patrols bonded as waterlogged friends.

"Thanks," offered Dave, as he happily helped his scouts out of the creek. "We'll probably see you guys later."

"You bet," returned his counterpart. "That was fun."

Later in the day, with dry uniforms on, the scouts gathered for a firearms demonstration put on by a state police officer. He had set up a portable backstop on the side of the hill. First the officer fired various handguns, hitting bulls-eye after bulls-eye on the targets. Then, firing a twelve-gauge shotgun, he demolished several targets at close range. Finally, pausing dramatically for effect, the officer opened a case and withdrew a .45 caliber Thompson submachine gun. The chattering scouts quieted instantly as they realized what was about to happen. Inserting a fresh magazine and charging a round, he pointed the weapon at the backstop and emptied the magazine in short bursts that sounded like a giant running a stick along a picket fence. As the empty cartridge cases flew through the air, they formed a metallic rainbow and landed near Steve's feet. When the firing stopped, the crashing noise continued in Steve's ears, the now-silent gun smoking in the officer's hands.

It was the first time that Steve had seen a Tommy gun. The noise of it had shaken him to the core. He was surprised when the officer pointed out that every bullet had struck the target. Reaching down to the grass, Steve retrieved one of the spent cartridges and slipped it into his pocket, a souvenir that he would keep for years.

On Sunday morning, after the camp-wide church service, awards were presented to the troops, recognizing their weekend achievements. With pride, Max watched as Pierre accepted a blue ribbon to display on their troop flag. It would join dozens of others earned over the years, that, even now, fluttered in the breeze. It was one of three given to outstanding troops at the camporee. Max's patrol leaders had done their jobs well. The training had paid off. Troops 35 was again in the limelight.

Max the Man

"Load 'em up," Bob bellowed when the appointed hour arrived. As Bob, his bald pate gleaming in the sun, clambered into the cab, his boys hopped in the back of the '37 General Motors truck for the jolting ride to the river bottom where they were going to begin their day-long hike. There were six boys altogether, and they held on tightly to any protuberance available in the back of the truck.

Quickly leaving the gravel roads of town, Bob headed down the rutted back road that precariously crossed a swamp. The road skirted cedar trees growing in standing water surrounded by areas of thick, clinging mud. A vehicle leaving the path would rapidly settle in the mire until the headlights were barely visible. It soon became a mere track that wandered around obstacles, trying desperately to stay on the high ground, but with only limited success. In some places cedar logs had been sawed to appropriate lengths and corduroyed across the low-lying ground. The trail wandered erratically before ending at a precipitous drop to the river.

They travelled five miles after leaving the edge of town. In that time they had not seen a single house. Their intention was to hike along the river, following ancient Indian and animal paths until they returned to town. Following the river as it meandered around hills and through a forest, their route was at least ten miles long. They would probably not see another person for many hours. It was the way they liked to hike because they were Boy Scouts. Bob was the scoutmaster and Max was one of the oldest boys in the troop.

Usually the crystal-clear river ran deep and swift, but

occasionally cascaded over shallow rocks with the abandon of wild white water. Weed banks undulated gracefully in the swift current and were home to many trout. Sunken logs were clearly visible through eight feet of water. Water fowl flourished along its banks: ducks, coots, herons, bitterns, rails, and gulls. The fluted head of a wood duck could be seen poking out of a hole high up a tree where it built its nest to avoid predators. Kingfishers roamed the sky, searching for small fish. When one was spotted, the Kingfisher would fold its wings and fall towards the river, detonating the river's surface as the Kingfisher grabbed its dinner. Its happy song was pleasant company to scouts hiking along the river.

It was to be Max's last hike with the troop. He was seventeen years old and would soon be leaving for the Merchant Marines. As he hiked along the river that day, Max thought back on all of his years in the troop. He thought of his experiences in First Aid, Life Saving, Personal Health, Public Health, Cooking, Camping, Civics, Bird Study, Path Finding, Safety, Pioneering, and Athletics, the required merit badges he had earned to become an Eagle scout. While earning them he had rubbed shoulders with great men, experts in their fields, who had taught him much and helped him to discover more. Scouting had been good to him he realized, and he owed a debt to scouting that he would someday need to repay.

Too quickly the hike was over, a pleasant footnote in Max's book of scouting memories. Never again would Max enjoy nature's splendor as a youth. Duty called and he would leave behind his beloved north woods. Max would have to focus on learning the skills of life aboard a ship as it sailed the oceans of the world under a sky that stretched across the horizon.

When the war started, following the attack at Pearl Harbor, Max transferred to the Navy. He spent the war years on a PT boat in the southwest Pacific Ocean. During quiet evenings, as he awaited contact with the enemy of his country, Max became more cognizant of the value of what he had learned as a scout.

He thought about the Scout Law, those twelve critical

attributes of a scout's life. He remembered hearing his scoutmaster tell him that the law said "A Scout *is* trustworthy...A Scout *is* loyal..." and so on. A scout didn't hope to be trustworthy at some point in the future. He wasn't loyal only on Scout day or while in uniform. He was trustworthy and loyal always. If he valued the ideals of scouting, a boy lived them full time. That's what Max did throughout the war. His standards were different from the other sailors, and his life reflected that.

Returning home from the war, he entered the dairy business. From dairy farmers, he collected raw milk, which he processed and packaged before delivering it to homes and stores. He had a small fleet of delivery and service trucks for his dairy, which, over the years, came in quite handy for scouting trips.

He met and courted Lillian, who came from a closely knit family of Italian Catholics. With Lil, Max found ties that had been missing in his own family. Together they started a family of three sons and a beautiful daughter. Life seemed good for the Bauer family; they had a nice house, great kids, a good livelihood, and a tightly woven family. The only thing missing was scouting. Max remembered his last hike along the river before going to sea and the realization he had had concerning the debt he owed to scouting. He became a scoutmaster, a capacity he ably filled for thirty-three years.

Sand Dunes

According to the legend, a mother bear and her cubs decided to swim across the lake. The cubs eagerly frolicked in the water that was deep blue, its coolness refreshing to the family of bears. Not realizing the size of the lake, mother bear swam until the shore was lost from view. Following her instinct, she continued on with the wind at her back, the cubs losing some of their friskiness as they began to fall behind, paddling desperately to keep their mother in sight. As the sun set on the bear trio, they were no longer together, the cubs having fallen far behind. The survival instinct drove the mother bear ever eastward. Through the night, she continued paddling until, near exhaustion, she stumbled onto the sandy bottom of the lake as the sky lightened ahead of her. The mother bear staggered to the safety of the beach. There she collapsed, facing westward, her head resting on her outstretched paws as she waited patiently for her cubs to reach the shore. Unknown to her, both cubs had slipped silently beneath the surface of the water within moments of each other, neither having the strength to continue the marathon swim.

Exhausted and bereft, her heart broken, the mother bear slipped away from consciousness, her last thought for her cubs that were lost on the vastness of the lake. An evening breeze ruffled her brown fur as it deposited beach sand along her downwind side. Eventually, in death, the legend continued, she was covered with a sand dune, which grew in size as a monument to her mother's love. Covering grasses along the lake and, ultimately, the trees that grew along the shoreline as well, the sand marched resolutely inland, claiming more territory through the empty halls of time.

When Max took his troop to that area, the sand dunes covered a vast tract of land, a virtual desert along a mighty lake. The sand covering the bear had risen several hundred vertical feet and extended inland for five miles or more, claiming land at the rate of ten feet per year.

His scouts set up their tents at the base of the sand dunes, which towered two hundred feet above them before curving out of sight to the west. In sheltered places grass grew in clumps, which struggled against the day-long searing wind and was anchored by the fine grained sand and clung there like landborne barnacles clinging tenaciously to an inverted sea's bottom. As the scouts set up camp, the sun was descending behind the sand dunes leaving elongated shadows of grass stretching down the hollows of sand, like long fingers pointing towards the scouts' homemade tents. A cooling evening breeze heralded the approach of a storm, but still carried on it the essence of parched sand. The vagrant breeze swept before it all traces of the passage of man. Footprints quickly filled in and any carelessly dropped bit of trash was hurried along the sand until it stuck in the grass near the bottom of the dune. The swirling winds worried the grass, sending the blades dancing in a circle, leaving an orbicular trail in the sand to mark the wind's passage.

Max reminded his scouts that, during a rainstorm, water tended to collect in low-lying areas. Mike promptly pitched his tent at the bottom of a small depression, proving to Max, once again, that it often takes several repetitions before a lesson is learned. And experience is often a better teacher than words alone. Since it would be a warm summertime rain, Max decided to let this night be a learning experience for Mike.

Around 10:00 P.M., the rains began in earnest, beating a steady tattoo on the fabric of Max's cabin tent: a warm weather tintinnabulation that lulled him effortlessly to sleep. As he slipped into a satisfied slumber, perched high above the ground on his army cot, a smile flickered briefly on his face as he wondered what time Mike would awaken him with the news that

21

his tent was awash and his cookies were soggy.

The porous sand could not soak up the rain as quickly as it fell and it began running down the face of the sand dunes and collecting in nearby concavities. The first things that floated out of Mike's tent were the individual boxes of cereal he was planning on eating for breakfast. They bobbed in the water like wayward buoys that had broken their moorings and floated away until touching the shore of Mike's pond where they lodged in the tall grass. At midnight, Mike awoke, having dreamt that he had been fishing and had fallen overboard while setting the hook in the mouth of a giant northern pike. Splashing in his sleeping bag, Mike realized that the dream had merged with reality. His tent buddy, Wilbur, was still wrapped in the soggy arms of sleep.

"Wilbur, wake up!" urged Mike. "Everything's soaked." No response. This time louder, "Wilbur, wake up!" Still no response.

Mike swam out of his sleeping bag and splashed his way to the tent door, which he untied with wrinkled fingers before sticking his head out in the rain. It didn't seem much wetter outside than it did in the tent. Even in the dark, Mike could tell that his was the only tent under water. Max's tent looked to be high and dry, the product of careful planning and years of experience. Now Mike understood what Max had tried to tell them when they set up camp.

Through the fog of sleep, a voice seemed to be calling to Max. He rubbed his eyes as he held his watch in front of his face, trying to read the luminous hands of time. It was just on the far side of midnight. "How high's the water, Mike?" shouted Max through the wall of his tent, knowing it would be Mike's voice that answered his query.

"Six inches," came the soggy reply. "What should I do?"

"Wake up your patrol leader. Have him help you move your tent to high ground. If you need more help, wake up Pierre. He would like to hear from you tonight. Call me if you need more help," added Max. He shone his light on a thermometer he kept near his cot. It read 68° so he knew that Mike would not have too many problems for the rest of his learning night.

In the morning, Max reminded the scouts to spread their gear out in the early sunlight, giving it a chance to dry in the heat of the day. The storm had ended just as Mike finished moving his tent. John, his patrol leader, had been less than pleased with Mike's request for help until he realized that, as patrol leader, he should not have let Mike set up his tent where he did.

After breakfast, Max and Pierre led the troop up the face of the sand dune. As they travelled in the morning stillness, the scouts noticed shadows on the sand created by small indentations in the early morning sun. Delicate feet had made twin tracks that arched across the sand before disappearing in the distance.

"What made them, Max?" questioned Mike, waving his arm vaguely in the direction where the tracks vanished.

"Let's follow them and see," offered Max, always looking for teaching moments.

Within minutes the scouts came upon a large black beetle, ponderously walking on stiltlike legs like a sailor on his first day ashore following a long voyage at sea. Each foot left a tiny imprint: an Amphitritean necklace in the wet sand. When Mike extended his hand toward the beetle, it stopped and leaned back on its hind legs, enormous armored pincers raised in an aggressive defensive posture. The beetle looked as if it could snap its pincers closed on an extended finger and remove a substantial pound of flesh from a victim. Wisely, Mike retreated. Satisfied, the beetle, its back the color of a smoky cauldron, resumed its march towards the far horizon, victor again in a battle with giants, invincible in its bantam universe.

Several hours later, with only sand visible wherever the scouts looked, Max called a pause in the hike to check his bearings. The morning sun had slipped behind hazy clouds, creating a flat light that made direction finding difficult for those depending on the sun. The gentle morning breeze had changed to a moderate wind that wildly gyrated the clumps of sea grass, making them near lethal scythes mowing in the fields of scout legs. The heat, though not overpowering, was enough to dehydrate the scouts who were depending on the cool waters of the lake to quench their thirst. Pierre was content to leave route-finding to Max.

"Which way do we go, Pierre?" asked Max, who wanted to keep his senior patrol leader tuned in and tightened down.

Pierre glanced at the overcast sky, looking for a directional clue. The sun appeared to be directly overhead, but it was hard to tell for certain. His watch told him it was almost noon. So no help from shadows. Sneaking a look at a nearby hill, Pierre said, "Wait here. I'll be right back."

Jogging up the hill, which was the tallest one around, Pierre thought he could find his location from his lofty vantage point. When he reached the top, Pierre stopped, slightly winded, and looked around him. For three directions there was nothing visible but sand. Looking behind him, Pierre hit pay-dirt. The lake stretched to the horizon, an endless cobalt blue. "We need to go that way," shouted Pierre as he gestured to the west.

"I agree," replied Max, as he returned his compass to his shirt pocket and headed around the hill that Pierre had climbed. "If you are lost, try to climb something tall to regain your bearings," he offered the rest of the scouts. "Or use the compass that you should always carry."

When they reached the shoreline, all of the scouts peeled off everything except their shorts and splashed into the lake, throwing water everywhere in their haste to rehydrate. Max, leaning on his trident hiking stick, looked like a modern Neptune as he surveyed his flock of scouts, satisfied that they were happy, safe, and still learning.

Pine River Bridge

The Pine River rambled over gravel beds and rocky outcrops, providing many stretches of white water for canoeists during several days of travel through the hills and forests of the central part of the state. Max and his scouts had several times taken three-day trips down the river. During those trips they rarely saw other people unless the strangers were also in canoes. No towns were located along the river and few homes dotted the riverbanks.

Pierre suggested a camping trip to the banks of the river to enjoy fishing, bird and wildlife study, and a chance to go hiking. Pierre found it rather tedious sitting on his backside in a canoe while he floated past mile after mile of virgin hiking country. The rest of the boys agreed on the trip, so the scouts were dropped off near a bridge that crossed far above the deep, swiftly flowing river. Forever after, in the legends of Pierre, it was remembered as the Pine River Bridge trip.

Steve was a new scout then. It was his first warm-weather camping trip. He was impressed when Max built his warming fire. Max carefully cut his kindling into small slivers. He had earlier gathered the dry bark from a birch tree and crumpled it up. Placing the ball of bark in the center of his river rock fire ring, Max delicately balanced the slivers of kindling on top, explaining that a fire must be constructed from small pieces to gradually increasing larger pieces. His slivers of kindling were built in a tepee shape. To the top of the sliver tepee, Max added larger pieces of kindling: first, pieces the size of a small finger and then some thumb-sized pieces. Steve carefully watched all of Max's preparations because he knew that a good scout should be able to light such a fire with only one or, at most, two matches. He wanted to be able to build a fire as Max did. It certainly looked like a good foundation for a fire. Then Max got out a red can, the same can that held the fuel for his Coleman lantern. From it he poured a small amount of liquid onto the top of his carefully built tepee.

"Get back!" ordered Max, as he struck a match on the zipper of his pants. Tossing the match on the firewood, Max was pleased when, with a whoosh, his fire ignited quickly, burning merrily in the dark as frogs chirped their night songs along the bank of the river.

Seeing the surprised look on Steve's face, Max offered, "I'm an Eagle scout. I have been for a long time. Many times I have proven that I can light a fire with only one match. It's easier this way. When you are an Eagle scout, you, too, can light a fire this way."

As Steve wrestled with the notion of a scoutmaster building a fire with white gas, he decided that, for the time being, example was a good idea. His fires would be built the way Baden-Powell taught: without an accelerant.

After the songs and stories around the campfire, Steve crawled into his sleeping bag. Since the night was warm and it didn't look like rain, Steve had rolled his bag onto the hard ground with only a tarp under him. It was an army surplus wool-lined mummy bag that his parents had picked up for five dollars from an older boy in the troop. As long as the nights were warm, the bag kept him warm, but scratched viciously all night long. During winter weather, Steve was cold all night long, itching and shivering the night away. He rested on his back, hands interlocked behind his head, as he lay on the riverbank, watching the canopy of diamond-white stars sparkling overhead. Occasionally, a shooting star would blaze across the sky, leaving a luminescent streak to mark its passage across the heavens.

Steve decided that he wanted to be like Max. He was going to get as many of his Tenderfoot requirements passed as he could during their three days along the river. He wanted to, someday, be an Eagle scout. Sometime later, as Steve fantasized about becoming a Star scout, he fell asleep. Finding a comfortable position was hard to do even while asleep. As he dreamed of scouting adventures, Steve rolled over, tossing in his sleep.

Steve did not realize that he was sleeping in a path regularly used by creatures of the night. In his dream, Steve was transported to a creek near his home: one frequented by raccoons who regularly visited its banks at night looking for dinner. Thinking a coon had run over him on the way to the creek, Steve jerked awake sitting upright, wide-eyed but still groggy with sleep. He realized that he was stuck partway out of his bag and that the zipper was behind him in the middle of his bag where he couldn't reach it. Steve had an acute case of claustrophobia.

He twisted around, trying to get to his zipper, when, in the glow of the stars, he saw the critter that had run over him while he slept. Too late, he realized it wasn't a coon when he saw the distinctive black shape with a white stripe running down the length of its back. Apparently, when Steve was thrashing around trying to extricate himself from the grasp of his suffocating sleeping bag, he had startled the beast. From a distance of twenty feet, the skunk pointed its business end at Steve and raised its tail before firing a blast of the most odoriferous substance Steve had ever encountered. It enveloped him in a cloying, clinging cloud of curdled air.

With tears streaming from sightless eyes, Steve rolled over and over, gagging as he went, until, with a plop, he fell from the bank into the river. He was still trapped in his sleeping bag, which seemed imminently to become a pungent riparian coffin. Fortunately, Max heard the commotion outside his tent and stuck his head out just as Steve rolled past, leaving a miasma of skunk essence in his wake. Max reached Steve just as he started to float away. Dragging Steve back to the safety of the shore, Max fell to his knees as the aroma hit him with full force.

Thinking quickly, Max unzipped the sleeping bag and

27

shoved both the bag and Steve back into the river. Dashing back to his tent, Max retrieved a bottle of liquid dish soap. From a safe distance, he threw it at Steve.

"And don't come back until you smell like a rose."

For an hour Steve scrubbed, wearing off the nap of the sleeping bag and rubbing his skin raw. He washed his hair several times, but the odor stayed in his nose. It seemed impossible to remove it completely. Max built up his fire and gathered a large supply of wood for Steve. Together they strung up the soggy sleeping bag on a rope stretched between two trees and hanging near the fire. Steve then sat by the fire, huddled in a wool army blanket that Max had thoughtfully added to his pack. It was rough as a cob, but it kept Steve warm. He kept the fire going for several hours until his bag had dried enough for him to crawl back into to catch a few hours of restless sleep.

The next day the rest of the scouts teased Steve about being such a good friend to animals. They figured that the skunk liked Steve so well that, on the spot, it baptized Steve a member of the skunk fraternity. Steve took the teasing with good humor. Fortunately, his uniform had been in his pack during the vicious attack and had not been hosed down by the night visitor. With time, Steve got used to the residual odor and hardly noticed it.

According to the map, there was another bridge about five miles downstream. Pierre would lead the troop on a hike down the right bank of the river, come out at the next bridge, and follow the highway back to camp. Along the way, they would identify plants, animals, and birds.

Leaving the camp behind, Pierre ordered a quiet march. As they rounded each river bend, startled water fowl flashed into the air, with wings churning the water to foam as the birds frantically flapped their wings trying desperately to avoid the two-legged intruders. The scouts flushed mallards, teal, gadwalls, and pin-tails. Wood ducks, goldeneyes, canvas backs, and mergansers flashed into the sky ahead of them. Great blue herons startled the scouts as they beat the air with enormous wings, ponderously rising into the air before exiting on graceful wings that seemed to move in slow motion. Ruby-throated hummingbirds flashed through the air, squeaking as they flew, their gossamer wings visible only when the sun reflected rainbows to watching eyes.

Hairy and downy woodpeckers beat a tatoo on tree trunks as they searched for eight-legged meals. Wood-peewees dive-bombed the scouts, snapping their wings near the scouts heads when they approached too closely to the family nest. Swallows and martins patrolled the river, eating enormous numbers of insects and skimming the river, sipping water in flight. Once, the scouts flushed a long-eared owl from its daytime perch, long before it began its nocturnal prowl for dinner. It lumbered into the air before dodging through the trees, looking for quieter surroundings for its afternoon slumber.

The scouts spotted two porcupines waddling along the river, with barbed skewers clanking along behind. They saw several kinds of squirrels, a few rabbits, and a bald-faced opossum wandering along an animal trail with its young hanging from its tail. They discovered muskrats swimming along the river, their bare tails motoring in their wake, and watched them dive to the entrance of their riverbank abode. Several deer bounded away, the white flags of their tails bobbing through the trees before they disappeared over a hill. Once the scouts found some cat tracks in the mud of the riverbank. The tracks were much larger than those of a house cat. Pierre told the scouts that the tracks were made by a bob cat prowling around during the previous night. They did not see any more skunks.

The hours passed quickly as the scouts learned about the feathered and furry friends of the forest. All too soon, the scouts found themselves at the bridge that marked their point of return. After a short rest, in the coolness of its shade, Pierre led the boys up the bank and onto the old county road that they would follow back to camp.

After walking a short distance from the road, Pierre had an overpowering urge to void his bladder.

"I've never peed in a road before," he announced, unzip-

29

ping his fly. "Line up by patrols in the center of the road."

In unison, all of the scouts in the troop aimed their yellow streams at the highway where they blended with the center line, glistening in the setting sun.

"Ah!" exclaimed Pierre. "Another of life's goals is now behind me!"

He then pivoted on his right foot and headed back to camp, singing hiking songs at the top of his voice. The other scouts joined in, hoping to improve on the quality of the melody and trying not to offend any listening ears.

Spider Lake

The lake on which Max took his scouts camping one spring was one of many in the region. The main part of the body of water was roughly ovoid in shape. Rearing up near the south end of it was a stately, uninhabited island about two acres in size. As far as anyone knew, the island was unnamed. The lake had many inlets scattered semi-evenly around its shore. Some of the bays sheltered homes that were summer getaways for people from the southern part of the state who had incomes sufficient to afford a second home. From the air, that particular lake had the appearance of a benevolent arachnid and was thus named Spider Lake.

During the summer the waters of Spider Lake were tepid. It was a small lake, perhaps two miles across, and, because it was sheltered by the old pines that surrounded it, was usually placid, even on days when the wind blew through the tops of the trees. In some of its tucked-away corners, lily pads flourished. Those broad flat water leaves undulated with the rippling of the water. Their starkly white flowers were a brilliant contrast to the deep emerald of the pads. Birds hopped about on them, looking for hatching insects to masticate. The pads were also frequent resting stops for passing frogs. Beneath them lurked several kinds of bass, sun fish, blue gills, and muskies: the barracudas of northern lakes. The fish had found the lily pads to be productive dining areas.

On calm days, painted turtles poked their snouts well above the water as they floated on the surface, sunning themselves. Their smooth dark green carapaces were a pleasant divergence from the many hues of their undercarriage. Snap-

31

ping turtles dwelt there also, though less abundantly than the painted turtles. The shell of an old snapper was convoluted, like worn-down mountains crowded into close proximity. There were some old moss-backed snappers in the lake that could cleanly sever the finger of an unwary scout who dangled a digit too closely to its maws, so it was important to distinguish between the two if a person attempted to catch a turtle.

The croaking of bull frogs and the higher trills of spring peepers announced the setting of the sun. Their soporific melodies carried far into the night, smoothing the rough edges of night listeners. On most evenings, hoot owls roamed the forest nearby, often in pairs, though most commonly on solitary expeditions. Their hooting in the shank of the night was both a warning to unwary ground dwellers and a talisman of luck for tired scouts.

Two pairs of loons made their summer homes in secluded corners of the lake. They could be seen riding low in the water, their black-and-white checkered backs looking like camouflaged submarines riding low on the water. With their long black beaks, they fished for underwater dinners during their long graceful dives. They seemed to accept human company as long as the scouts didn't approach too closely.

In the evenings, fireflies, those ubiquitous lanterns of the night, helicoptered through the trees at the margins of the lake. In slow motion they glided through the night, their tails lambent in the quiescent air. Max loved the fireflies. They reminded him of the campfires of a thousand nights camping with scouts. Each evening the scouts would gather around the fire, singing songs and telling stories while enjoying a spirit of brotherhood. As the evening waned and the songs mellowed with the night, the collapsing logs of the fire shot embers heavenward like the dreams of a thousand boys. Max thought of the fireflies as nocturnal embodiments of the embers of those long-ago campfires and long-ago dreams.

Max had a canoe. It was made of canvas-covered wood. On the inside, the ribs, thwarts, planking, and seats gleamed with many coats of marine varnish. Woven wicker seats added a touch of old-time voyagers to the canoe. Its most distinguishing feature, though, was its outer surface. Max had painted the canvas a flat white, over which he added black paint to make it look like the pitched-over seams of a birch bark canoe. It looked delicate, as if a strong wave might collapse its hull, but was surprisingly sturdy.

After taps one night, the older scouts slipped silently from camp and gathered at the shore where Max's canoe had been beached for the night. Roy, one of the Beavers, dropped a length of rope in the front of the canoe.

Some of the boys lifted the canoe from its resting place and slid it silently into the still water. Steve, from the Eagle patrol, was an expert canoeist, so he carefully boarded the canoe and stealthily paddled it farther down the shore where the rest of the older scouts had quietly donned their swimming suits.

One of the skills that Max had taught his boys was commando swimming. Making only a whisper of sound, they entered the water, and without making a ripple, headed for the island, which was about three hundred yards offshore. Because sound travelled so well across the water, especially at night, the scouts travelled without talking for the twenty minutes required to make the crossing. Steve paddled the canoe noiselessly alongside in case any scout ran into difficulty.

John was a strong swimmer but hated underwater plants. He imagined the long-clinging water weeds as the tentacles of freshwater octupi. He could feel the rough edges of the plants brushing against his legs as he swam along. But when he neared the shore, John swam into a huge bed of weeds. He panicked as he felt the plants grasping his shoulders, their weight seeming to drag him bottomward. By forcing his mind to think of other things, John was able to finish the crossing safely. He swam until his chest gratefully brushed the bottom of the lake, then, like Neptune, he rose to his feet, water streaming down his legs and vines hanging from his shoulders. With a shudder, John cast away the weeds as a spasm of relief coursed up his spine. He decided to ride back with Steve.

As Roy crossed, he thought about making a raft out of logs

that lay in abundance on the island. Lashing was one of his specialties, and he knew that in an hour or so, he could fashion a platform of logs that should support his weight. He imagined himself to be a modern-day Huck Finn and would proudly float back to the shore on his Mississippi raft. He had tossed the rope in the canoe for that purpose.

As they gathered near the shore of the island, congratulating themselves on the success and audacity of their mission, a bright light flashed across the lake from their camp. All of the boys dove for cover, not wanting to be visible in the glare of Max's light. As he dove for cover, Roy felt a searing pain in his left wrist. It felt as if a giant had stuck a knife in the soft part of Roy's inner wrist. Pain shot upwards like the time he had grabbed an electric fence on a dare. Only this pain was infinitely worse.

"All right, you guys. Get back over here!" It was Max. He sounded like he knew they were on the island, but he didn't seem mad.

"Lie still. Maybe he won't see us," offered John. "He can't know we're here. We were too quiet coming over."

"I'm hurt," groaned Roy. "It's my left wrist. It feels like I have something sticking in it. I need to get back to shore so I can do first aid on myself." Roy was one of the guys the scouts depended on for first-aid instruction. He knew about pressure points and how to use a cravat as a bandage.

The light had been sweeping back and forth along the shore of the island. Max seemed to know what he was looking for. Then the beam of light stopped right on the canoe, pinning it to the shore like an insect mounted for display. As they watched from the underbrush, the scouts were dismayed to see a second light, this one Max's huge two-cell camp lantern bobbing along towards the other now-motionless light. Max must have set down the first one and returned to his tent to get his big light. Both were focused on the canoe.

"You can come back now, fellers," Max called across the tranquillity of the evening. "I don't want to have to swim over there to get you."

Sheepishly, the scouts straggled to their feet and shuffled towards the water's edge. Roy was holding his wrist tightly against his chest. Even in the darkness, his face looked pale.

"Hop in the canoe, Roy," ordered John. To the rest of the scouts, he said, "The three of us will spot you back to the mainland." He wasn't getting back in that weed-infested lake for anything.

Max lighted the way for them. Roy's wrist was throbbing with each stroke of Steve's paddle. He was lying on the bottom of the canoe with his feet propped up so they were higher than his head. For him time seemed to have stopped. The night had become quiet as if the lantern's illumination had been a signal of silence for the night creatures.

"What did you guys think you were doing?" questioned Max, as the group neared the shore. "Never mind, I don't really want to know. I wish you had let me know you were going."

"Roy's hurt," offered John. "Something's wrong with his wrist," he said as the canoe scrapped gently on the sandy beach.

"Let's take a look at it," Max said, handing the lantern to John. As John aimed the light at Roy's wrist, Max was able to see ragged edges of wood protruding from the skin. Several huge slivers had embedded themselves deeply in Roy's wrist. "We'd better get up to the tent so we can work on him. Steve, make sure the canoe is high and dry. The rest of you hit the sack. I don't want to see or hear you again until breakfast.

"Sit there by the lantern," instructed Max, as they reached his tent. "Let's see, now where is my saw?" he asked as he carefully watched for a response from Roy? When he got no reaction, Max went to his tent for the first-aid kit.

"Let me help," volunteered John. "My dad's a doc. I know what to do." With that, John picked up a stick from near his feet, and, holding it between his thumb and forefinger, used it as a crude tweezers. He was able to grasp the end of one splinter, but in doing so, he drove other splinters farther into the tender flesh of Roy's wrist.

With a scream, Roy jerked away from Good Samaritan

John and clutched his injured wrist close to his chest.

"Gee, I'm sorry, Roy," said John apologetically. "You need to hold still while I'm working on you. How am I going to get the slivers out if you keep jerking away?"

"Keep away from me, you butcher," retorted Roy, as he stalked into the tent after Max. Sitting on the edge of Max's cot, Roy gingerly offered his wrist for Max's scrutiny.

"This looks pretty serious, Roy. I'm afraid the best I can do is wrap it up for you. In the morning I will take you to the hospital."

Through the rest of the night, Roy tossed and turned in his sleeping bag, the dull pain in his wrist turning to fire. Sleep was impossible for him. His dream of floating across the lake had become a nightmare of agony.

By morning, his wrist was angry with color, swollen and very painful. Max had the rest of the scouts break camp early and everything was loaded into the old delivery truck by 8:00 A.M. The canoe was lashed to the top of the vehicle and scouts were perched precariously on packs, boxes, and equipment sacks inside. The hospital was twenty miles away but seemed farther because of the serpentine road.

After an interminable interlude on the road, Roy was finally ushered in to see a real doc. He was whisked into a treatment room, where his wrist was disinfected and a local anesthetic was administered to dull the pain. The doctor probed and pulled as he removed the bits of wood that had been lodged deeply in Roy's wrist. The agony was caused, the doctor said, because one splinter was resting against a nerve. Fortunately, the nerve hadn't been damaged. After a thorough cleaning of his wound, Roy received a tetanus shot before wobbling back outside to rejoin his worried, waiting buddies.

Pounding him on the back, the other scouts in the troop shared with Roy a sense of relief that the damage was relatively minimal. As they turned towards Max, they knew that now was the time to face his wrath for pulling the stunt they had the previous evening.

"What did you learn, scouts?" inquired Max.

"Not to sneak off without telling you," said Steve, squirming as he avoided Max's steady gaze.

"Never try to remove an impaled object," offered would-be-doctor John sagaciously.

"It's too bad Pierre isn't with us," concluded Roy. "If he had been, we would have gone on a hike instead. We would have been too tired from the hike to swim across to the island."

Max nearly fell off his chair. "Did I hear you bandits, right? You actually miss Pierre and his hikes? You'd better not let him hear you say that. He might think you like him!"

Historic Trails

The Green Bar leaders planned a hike along a historical trail. Over a hundred years had passed since the trail had been used by the original explorers. They decided to follow a section of the path that was presently covered by a seldom-travelled gravel road.

There were three patrols in the troop then. The most experienced of them were the Eagles. Dave was the patrol leader. He had just earned his Life badge. His youngest charge was a Tenderfoot. The other boys in the patrol were either Second- or First-Class scouts. They had camped and hiked together for years.

The Beaver patrol was led by John, the son of a prominent doctor. John was nicknamed Jack, and he got a kick out of pretending he had a twin brother. "Hi, John," someone would holler in greeting.

"I'm not John. I'm Jack," he would shout back. "John couldn't be here today." He had many scouts believing there were actually two of him running around loose, especially when he was on camp staff and had a captive audience to work with all week.

Following John's example, the Beavers were a bunch of clowns. Always looking for a practical joke to play on others, they expended enormous energy trying to keep the rest of the troop from taking themselves too seriously. Late one evening on a winter camp, they unceremoniously tossed a screaming scout from another patrol into a handy snowbank. In the process of tossing him through the air, they managed to separate Jim from his pajamas. For lightly less than a nanosecond,

Jim lay on his back, naked and spread-eagled in the snow. He then shot straight up into the blackness of the night, executed a perfect ninety-degree turn in mid-air, and bolted back into his sleeping bag touching neither ground nor fabric in the process. He looked like a slightly blue, malevolent woodcock as he maneuvered through the sky. He swore dire and immediate vengeance upon all Beavers, but he took so long to warm up in his army surplus sleeping bag that he developed a case of temporary amnesia and never followed through with his promise of retaliation.

Gary was a First Class scout and patrol leader of the Flaming Arrow patrol. His patrol labored under the delusion that they were the best cooks in camp. On an earlier excursion, Larry, one of the Flaming Arrows, was warming up some beans for lunch. The patrol members had been practicing their skills for the Klondike Derby and had worked up a real appetite. They had pushed their sled across Cedar Lake, which was covered with two feet of ice and about as much snow. Once across the lake, they had practiced first aid and fire rescue along the bluffs overlooking the east side of the lake. Larry had taken a few of the boys ahead to practice fire-starting. They had a great cooking fire going by the time the rest of the patrol arrived. It was the kind of fire that used the better part of a cord of wood and roared high enough to singe the needles on a pine tree twenty feet in the air. It was a real scout fire and would have been just right for Sam McGee. As the rest of the boys approached, Larry said the beans were about done. Not wanting to get cooked himself, Gary searched the margins of the fire from a safe distance, but he could see no evidence of a pot or a pan.

"I forgot the opener," Larry said. "So I just set the can by the fire. It's sitting on that rock," he continued, pointing vaguely in the direction of the far side of the conflagration.

Gary grabbed two boys nearest him and ducked behind a pine tree, shouting at the rest of the boys to follow him. Through the grime on Larry's face, Gary could see that the blood had drained from it. "What's wrong with...," Larry

39

demanded when the quiet was shattered by a tremendous blast.

Peering around the tree, they could see smoldering cord wood scattered over a vast area. The fire was out. The bark from nearby trees had been stripped cleanly away and a few beans drizzled forlornly down the naked wood. The lid from the can was stuck in a nearby poplar tree, but the rest of it had disappeared.

"Never," Gary groaned. "Absolutely never should you put an unopened can of anything near a fire. You see what happens when you do?"

Larry gazed in wonder at what had been his cooking fire. A tear threatened to roll down his cheek. Mucus dripped from his nose, which he wiped on the back of his coat sleeve. He started to respond, stopped, and stared at the devastation caused by his culinary shenanigans. He looked like a beached fish gasping for air before finally blurting out, "And I thought beans popped only *after* you ate them."

Max gathered the boys together before they started out on their hike. "Remember to stay together as we hike. Don't spread out on the trail. Senior Patrol Leader, we should take a break every hour or so."

"Got it," replied Tom. "Eagle Patrol lead out, then Beavers, and finally the Flaming Arrows. Stay on the left side and keep together."

Since Max was with them, the boys in the troop really didn't worry about being on a trek with Tom. The road they were following led directly to the camping area they would use about twelve miles away.

Tom lit out like a scalded cat. He didn't even look back. In short order the troop was strung out over several hundred yards of trail. Max began muttering about staying together and trying to have tail-end Charlie, the Flaming Arrows, pick up the pace. Tom was out of sight.

They tried to practice their tracking skills as they moved along the trail, seeking to make sense out of the stories left in the dirt. They passed a stream and found a spot where some raccoons had stopped to catch minnows, their delicate tracks planted firmly in the stream-bank mud. They found the scattered feathers left when a hawk had snatched its meal from mid-air before perching on an overhanging branch near the trail to tear it apart. At one point they glimpsed the white-tipped tail of a red fox that was sneaking between some distant white birch trees. The fox was intent upon following an unseen trail and paid the boys no heed.

They saw a large brown bird, hopping up a tree, doing a vertical ballet. Its head was shaped like a woodpecker's and when it flew to another tree, the boys could see a patch of white feathers on its back.

"It's a flicker," Max told them. "A member of the woodpecker family. Like the Flaming Arrows, it prefers to eat whatever it finds while rummaging around."

After an hour, the scouts finally caught up with Tom, who told them that he had been waiting for ten minutes before they showed up. At least he wasn't lost. Max took him aside and had a few words with Tom. It probably had something to do with staying together as a group.

After the break the scouts continued down the trail. They found a place where beavers had been working. One fifteen-inch poplar stump had been cut off about five feet above the ground. Below that were two more notches, the first about two feet above the ground and the other one about three feet up. Both notches had been chiseled by beaver teeth and were more than halfway through the tree trunk.

"It snowed," Max told them. "About a foot or so. The beaver tried to cut down the tree but stopped before the job was done. When he came back later, more snow had fallen, so he had to start over. He didn't finish then either and another storm came in before he was finally able to finish the job."

They talked then about sticking to a difficult job. "Imagine how long it must have taken the beaver to finish cutting down that tree?" Max challenged. "Think of the disappointment when the beaver came back to find all of his hard work buried in the snow. You Beavers need to live up to the lesson

41

in the example we see here before us."

Tom was gone again. Not having to worry about getting lost seemed to have fried his brains. When the troop finally caught up with Tom, Max didn't bother taking him aside to tell him that the senior patrol leader should lead by example and should not travel faster than the slowest boy in the troop.

"Stay with us," Max told Tom in a voice that commanded respect.

During the break, while Roy, one of the Beavers, distracted Tom, John and his buddies slipped some boulders into the top of Tom's pack without being caught.

"That ought to slow him down," said John chuckling, pleased with his latest prank.

"Let's move out," ordered Max. "And this time stay together!"

Max was just getting warmed up, telling about the history of the trail. They passed a crooked tree that looked like the letter z stuck sideways in the ground. Max told them that the tree had been a marker for Indians who portaged their canoes from a big lake to another smaller one nearby. Max reported that an old-timer, born before the turn of the century, had followed the same trail when he was a boy and had said that the bent tree had been there as long as he remembered.

About that time Max discovered that Tom was far ahead again. Telling the patrol leaders to catch up as fast as they could, Max left John in charge as he jogged down the trail to catch Tom. Shortly after, Max was lost from view as he rounded a distant corner. John said that he probably should have put more rocks in Tom's pack.

When the boys next saw them, Tom was standing in the middle of the trail with his head bowed forlornly. His hat was missing. Max was standing near the tall, broken remains of a lightning-struck tree by the side of the trail. His hands were grasping the tree trunk on either side about head high. Tom's hat was precariously perched on the summit of the broken tree. Max was trying to shake the trunk and looked as if he might pull it from the ground. His angry voice was sprinkled with some really interesting-sounding words, but the boys were too far away to understand what he was saying.

The patrols gathered at a respectful distance until Max's anger seemed to wane. Tom had not spoken a word but looked really uncomfortable. When Max finally realized that the troop had caught up, John questioned him about the tree stump and Tom's hat sitting on top of it.

"I have just chosen the tree stump to be the new senior patrol leader. The stump will listen at least as well as Tom," Max offered. "And it won't talk back or get lost." The first of the boys to recover from the gales of laughter that followed was John, who immediately began looking for some more rocks.

Christmas Camp

Each year during the holidays, Max and his troop held a winter session at the scout camp. The troop was able to use cabins reserved for camp staff members during the summer. Perched in the pines at the edge of a hill overlooking the lake, the cabins were a hundred yards or so from the scout lodge, which doubled as a dining hall. Snow was often piled up four or five feet deep between the cabins, so the scouts scraped out narrow passages through the snow, which were easy to negotiate in the daylight. At night they were slippery, cold, and offered marvelous endefilades from which to launch a snowball attack on an unsuspecting patrol.

On Friday night the troop provided several cases of pop, fifty pounds of unshelled peanuts, and a stack of sixteen-millimeter movies, beginning with Laurel and Hardy and going downhill from there. The neat thing about Friday night was that the boys could throw the peanut shells on the floor and not have to take care of the empty pop bottles. The unwritten rule was that no clean-up could be done until after breakfast on Saturday. Peanut shells were everywhere, as were empty pop bottles. As the snowbanks were so high, the scouts could easily gorge themselves, then stagger outside and throw up without worrying about cleaning up that mess either.

Max had enough movies to last until about three in the morning. For the rest of the night, Max turned the projector to reverse and the boys watched the movies backwards. The scouts dragged all of the stuffed chairs in the scout lodge near the stone fireplace, which was large enough to hold a whole cow. It provided the only heat in the building and December, in the northern woods, was a cold time to be without heat. Above the fireplace were plaques made by each year's Order of the Arrow members who had gone through the Vigil weekend. The plaques represented hundreds of years of service to scouting and were ignored by all of the scouts who were not Vigil members themselves.

By midnight, some of the younger scouts had returned to the cabins, having run out of steam and stomach space. They were not yet hardened to the ritual of an overnight pigout session. Each cabin held five bunk beds that surrounded a fuel-oil stove. The younger scouts were relegated to the top bunks by the older boys. There were two temperature zones in each cabin, boiling and freezing. Those on the top bunks were sweltering in their sleeping bags. Those on the bottom bunks looked for warm things to pile on their sleeping bags. No one thought of turning off the heat. Then everyone would freeze.

Pierre had shown the boys how to open up their mouths wide and lower the back of their throats, creating a small vacuum that sucked air into their stomachs. With the intake of enough air, an enormous belch could be generated by even the smallest boy. The older scouts stayed up all night, trying to consume more pop and peanuts than Pierre and seeing who could belch the loudest. Some of them even watched the movies.

In belching, Pierre was without peer. His belches seemed to curl up from his toes, pausing in his stomach long enough to expand in size before rumbling past his epiglottis and rolling out into the room. There they bounced off the ceiling and tumbled to the floor where they caromed off stationary objects before fading away in a whisper of sound. It was best not to be near him when Pierre belched because his breath was truly fearsome, bringing tears to the eyes of strong men. When Pierre belched, the noise seemed eternal. When he talked while belching, Pierre was entertaining, but it was the singing belch for which Pierre was most famous. He could do the chorus of "The Dummy Line" with only four intakes of air and not even be tired when he finished. Hearing Pierre belch *Taps* was enough to put anyone asleep. He could also eat prodigious amounts of peanuts and swallow an amazing volume of pop without even puking once.

Of course, Pierre loved to hike. With no sleep Friday night, Pierre decided a hike around the boundaries of the camp was in order on Saturday morning. It was five miles around the camp, and the borders were marked by blazes cut on the bark of trees. Other than internal camp roads, the scouts would cross no other highways during the entire hike.

Max sent Steve along with instructions to keep Pierre out of trouble.

"Please don't let him get lost this time," Max pleaded, as the scouts set out slogging through knee-deep snow. "I need you back by lunchtime."

On the far side of the camp, Pierre surprised everyone by still having boundary blazes in sight.

"Let's stop here for a rest," he said loftily, as he plopped down on the edge of a bluff overlooking a river deep in the valley.

Deciding to stretch out completely, Pierre leaned back in the snow and flung his arms out. Realizing that he was in the proper position to make a snow angel, Pierre waved his arms and legs in and out, up and down until he had the desired pattern. As he sat up to admire his artwork, the friction holding Pierre on the edge of the bluff disappeared. So did Pierre. Over the edge he went, looking like a berserk toboggan, completely out of control. Accelerating through some raspberry bushes, which slowed him up only long enough to remove some hide from his face, Pierre rocketed down the hill, barely avoiding a clump of river birch before disappearing into a willow thicket far down the hill.

Steve held his breath as he waited for Pierre to reappear on the far side of the willows. When he didn't, Steve headed down the hill, post-holing in the deep snow instead of making a rapid descent as Pierre had. It was hard work, even going downhill. The snow seemed to cling to his boots, holding him back. Halfway down, Steve noticed that the bushes were rattling and shaking. Like a modern-day Moses, Pierre's hands parted the willows and his face appeared, a smile splitting his broad, scratch-covered face.

"That sure was fun," he offered. "Let's do it again."

"I don't think that would be a good idea," responded Steve. "I promised Max I wouldn't let you get into trouble. Come on, the rest of the scouts are waiting at the top."

The trip back up the hill took much longer than the one going down. The soft, deep snow gave way as they tried to climb straight up the hill. For every two small steps up they made, Steve and Pierre slid back one large step. Only by traversing the hill's face could they successfully negotiate it and rejoin the other boys. It took a long time.

By the time the boundary hike was finished, Steve and Pierre were leaning on each other for support, both too tired to walk unaided. They stumbled back to the scout lodge looking like two skid row derelicts, singing an off-key version of "I'm Happy When I'm Hiking." But they hadn't gotten lost and they were only three hours late. The rest of the boys in the troop were feeling good. *Not bad*, thought Max, as he watched his boys come in from another Pierre hike.

The next day was Sunday. Max led his scouts in a nondenominational worship service. He talked to the scouts about the brotherhood of mankind and the importance of helping each other. He reminded the scouts of the troop's tradition of pinning the Tenderfoot pin on the scout shirt pocket upside down when it was presented. When the new Tenderfoot scout did a good turn for someone else, he was entitled to turn the pin upright, as a symbol of his commitment to do a good turn daily.

"That is not just for new Tenderfoot scouts," Max reminded them. "Every scout should symbolically turn his rank pin each day." He reminded the boys of the parable of the talents and how whatever the boys sowed, they would also reap.

As the Christmas camp wound down, Pierre presented a new coffee cup and a pipe to Max, reminders from the scouts of the high esteem in which they each held Max.

"To a lot of us, you are like a father as well as a friend and scoutmaster," explained Pierre. "We wanted to show you how much you mean to us."

"Let's get cleaned up and get out of here," responded Max. "You guys are going to make me sentimental."

Some time during that night, the scout lodge burned to the ground. By the next morning, all that was left of fifty years of history were the stone fireplace and chimney.

"It's sad," Max later told the council executive. "We put out the fire before we left and hauled the ashes outside. I don't know how it could have happened."

"Don't worry," he was told. "The logs next to the fireplace got really hot and started to smolder. You didn't notice because you had a fire going. It was an accident."

Max was sure the council would send him the bill for a new scout lodge since his troop had used the old one last. It was the last Christmas campout the troop was to have.

Ordeal Weekend

From the flint and steel held in the hands of a scout dressed in the finery of an Indian, a single spark fell. Steve watched the scout, who became an Indian in his mind. The Indian carefully nurtured the embryo of fire that he had created. Blowing gently on it, he turned the glow of the spark into a tiny fire, which he placed at the base of a tepee of kindling that sat atop a pile of wood stacked like a solid log cabin. He was lighting the council fire at the bottom of a bowl-shaped amphitheater at scout camp. Appropriately enough, the area was known as The Bowl.

Overhead the nighthawks were shrieking as they plummeted to capture insects in flight. Not a breeze stirred. Mosquitoes were held at bay with a liberal dose of eye-burning, nose-stinging 6–12 insect repellent.

Seated on logs that marched around the fire and up the hillside were scouts who were finding out about the Order of the Arrow, the brotherhood of honored campers in the Boy Scouts of America. Steve had been selected to be a member of the Order, an honor bestowed on him by his fellow scouts. To be chosen, a scout must have devoted several years to the troop, demonstrating good scouting skills and extending the hand of brotherhood in scouting to others. A scout must also be an exemplary camper and must have demonstrated positive outdoor etiquette. And then he must be chosen by troop members before he could be inducted into the Order.

Max was a member of the Order of the Arrow. All of the adult scouters who Steve knew were members of the order also. Most of the boys in the troop over the age of fourteen were

49

members. It seemed that just about everyone Steve really respected in scouting was in the Order of the Arrow. Now it was his turn.

After explaining that the Order was also known as the brotherhood of cheerful service and had its origins at Treasure Island in the early days of scouting, the guide told the scouts that membership was both honorary and voluntary. He called those who had been selected to form a circle around the camp-fire. He admonished them to be reverently silent. He proceeded around the circle, tapping each scout strongly on the shoulder once followed by two more firm taps.

They were then led from the circle, up the hill to a trail running around the camp and near several camping areas. Along the way each candidate collected his sleeping bag but no tent or other equipment. As they progressed along the trail, each scout was dropped off about a hundred yards from other lone scouts. Steve's area was at the bottom of a hill in a clearing that let him see a part of the vast spread of stars above. He was told to spread out his sleeping bag, crawl in, and get a good night's sleep. In the morning someone would be by to pick him up.

As he lay in the woods, Steve's imagination ran wild. He knew that a serious trick was being played on him. After he had crawled into his sleeping bag, he imagined that the guide had returned, collected the other scouts, and left him alone deep in the woods. Steve had no idea where he was or how to get anywhere near civilization. He listened to the wind sighing through the pine trees, the rush of it probably covering up the stealthy approach of a bobcat or wolverine. The rubbing of branches was caused by unseen, but vividly conjured creatures in the dark. It was Steve's first solo night in the woods.

Shooting stars blazed across the sky, leaving their phosphorescent trail to briefly mark their passage. Steve found the Pole Star and looked toward the horizon to see the eerie pulses of the Aurora Borealis, a sight that never failed to send shivery fingers racing up and down his spine.

As he concentrated on the sky, trying to shut out the fearsome sounds of the night, Steve noticed clouds rolling up from the northwest. The wind increased in volume and became a rush rather than a sigh. One by one the stars were blotted out. A storm was approaching and Steve had nothing between the elements and himself but a mummy sleeping bag, the only redeeming characteristic being that the inner layer was wool. It was very thin.

The first flash of lightning was a surprise. Steve had always hated lightning. When he was much younger, his uncle's barn had been struck by lightning and burned to the ground before the volunteer fire department could stop the blaze. At home Steve always hid his head under the pillow, squeezing his eyes tightly shut during thunderstorms. Though diminished by his pillow, the lights and sounds of a storm were frightening. Now he had neither a house nor a pillow to which he could flee for safety. The thunder that cracked almost immediately after the flash struck him dumfounded.

With a vengeance, the rain began to fall, first as large sprinkles, then as drops of water that hit the ground in quarter-sized explosions of liquid that quickly soaked Steve and turned the ground all around him into mud. As the lightning flashed, he could still see a red glow through his tightly closed eyelids and the wet brown wool of his sleeping bag. His hands pressed tightly over his ears, but he could still hear the ripping and crashing of the thunder. It seemed to shake the ground and rattle the trees. The night became a living stroboscope accompanied by a cacophony of sounds. Steve could hear the trees thrashing in the wind and dead limbs crashing to the ground.

He huddled in his sleeping bag, too frightened to move, thinking his chances of being struck by lightning were less if he remained motionless. Then he noticed the stream that was flowing down the trail and under his sleeping bag. While not very large, the stream reminded him that he was at the bottom of a small valley. He rolled over a couple of times so that he was farther up the gently sloping hill and out of the stream and tried desperately to shut out the noise, knowing that only sleep would release him from his fears. For much of the night, though, sleep eluded him.

Through the remainder of the night, the storm rattled around the sky. The lightning and thunder seemed the embodiment of two demented sea captains holding a naval gun battle across the horizon from each other with Steve in the middle. He would slip into the bliss of sleep only to jerk awake shivering, trying to roll up in a tighter ball to keep warm. The night seemed never-ending.

Towards dawn, in the coldest part of the night, the storm wandered away. A distant flash lit the sky but was too far away for Steve to hear the thunder. The wind died to a gentle breeze and the trees resumed their lullaby.

Steve finally fell into a deep sleep just before dawn, only to be awakened by his guide as the sun rose in the eastern sky. The guide seemed dry and rested. Behind him straggled a line of scouts who looked to be survivors from the sunken ships of the previous night's naval battle. They had been plucked from the ocean just before Steve had. As Steve started to ask what was going to happen next, the guide held his fingers to his lips, signaling silence, and beckoned Steve to follow him.

They followed the trail until it led to the dining hall where a huge fire roared in the stone fireplace. The soggy scouts warmed themselves as their clothes dried. They were served a hearty breakfast of hot chocolate followed by an orange. They were a tired, miserable lot. Steve still hadn't learned anything about the brotherhood of cheerful service, only how to survive a harrowing night. Steve was surprised that he had, in fact, survived. He thought that fear was lethal.

The candidates were then led back to The Bowl where they had been tapped out so very long ago. Was it only last night? They sat there as the sun heated the concave outdoor cathedral. Steve pondered what he had experienced during the storm. He considered the loneliness of the long, long night and of being cold and hungry. He reflected on the unfairness of being abandoned for the night. Why did the storm have to come on that night? Why hadn't the guide come to rescue him when the storm was so fierce? Why did he have to be so afraid? Then Steve realized the significance of what he had done. He *had* faced his worst nightmare. Though cold and uncomfortable, he hadn't grabbed his sleeping bag and run screaming for help. He had passed a very uncomfortable personal test, though not with flying colors. With astonishment Steve realized that, though it could be intimidating, fear was deadly only if you let it control you. The sun was heating him from without, but Steve's discoveries made him feel warmed from within. *He had done it.*

The candidates were told then about the day ahead of them. They would be working all day, improving various parts of the camp. The work would be arduous. They were reminded of their charge to remain silent, serving others without complaint. The day passed quickly. Lunch was a glass of lemonade and another orange. During their spare time, each candidate carved something from a bit of dead wood. Steve carved an arrow. Another scout fashioned a wooden chain with interlocking links. One adult created the miniature wooden head of a scout complete with hat.

As he worked, Steve was not distracted by conversation because of his vow of silence. Remaining mute provided an opportunity to ponder the principle of service. As he planted pine seedlings, Steve realized that he would probably never see them reach maturity. The knowledge that he had helped reforest a hillside would be his reward. Their shade would benefit others. Service then, was doing good things for others without hoping for recognition for his goodness or benefiting directly from its performance. The best kind of service, at least for Steve, was that given without others knowing that he had made a contribution, especially those for whom the service was rendered.

As the day ended, all of the tired scouts filed past a council fire. Each was instructed to add his own carving to the fire, symbolizing his sacrifice for others as he tried to be of service. Carving the arrow had not been difficult for Steve. At first the notion of consigning it to the flames was disconcerting to him.

He wanted to keep it as a symbol of having conquered his fear of darkness and storm. Then he realized that his memories of the weekend would be vivid and adequate. With only a pause in his step, as he reverently honored his creator with gratitude for the wisdom he had gained, Steve added his carving to the heat of the fire.

Maple Syrup

The railroad right-of-way had been abandoned for years. The tracks and ties had been salvaged and only the ballast remained to thwart Nature's reclamation project. Small trees were growing where freight trains had once labored, their buds threatening to burst with the warming of spring. Snow was still deep on the north-facing hillsides, but in the valleys facing the warm sun, the flattened leaves that had floated to the ground six months in the past were starting to dry out. Soon mushrooms would be sprouting among the fallen logs that were rotting as they completed the cycle of life.

Leather boots had been greased to keep out the moisture of melting snow. External frame scout backpacks were bulging with the gear necessary for three days in the woods. Steve, the senior patrol leader, carried a brace and bit for drilling and some wooden sprouts that were six inches long. Each patrol, in addition to its regular equipment, carried two ten-quart buckets. Max and his scouts were going camping in the sugar bush where they would tap some maple trees to capture the sap that had already begun to course through the trees in one of the first harbingers of spring.

For two miles they followed the trail made by the trains of old until they came to a section of the woods that grew on a south-facing hillside and was relatively free of snow. It was long after dark, and, even in the early springtime air, the temperature was near freezing.

Steve showed the patrol leaders where to set up their tents, those heavy cotton structures that leaked when it rained in spite of the water-proofing liquid the scouts added each spring. Each tent made almost a full load for one boy to carry and held four scouts in crowded comfort. Steve helped the boys set up their tents in the darkness, which was broken only by the umbrella of stars and a slowly rising moon overhead.

Billy was a new scout, one Steve had to watch closely. Billy's arms and legs seemed to be moving constantly, usually pulling off the hat of another scout before throwing it in a tree or tripping a passing scout who walked too close to Billy. There was never any doubt about what he was thinking because every thought that wandered through his mind came quickly out of Billy's mouth as if in a rush to be expressed. On a troop bike ride, Billy, looking like a modern-day Ichabod Crane, elbows flapping and knees banging his handlebars, his head rotating on a swivel, had ridden his bicycle smack into the bumper of a parked pickup truck.

Fortunately Billy didn't hurt the truck. Only his dignity was damaged and that only momentarily, so Billy climbed back on his bike and wobbled down the road, giving every indication that he was oblivious to what had just happened. He never uttered a word, neither epithet nor one of surprise, as if running into a truck was a common experience. Max and Steve had been riding immediately behind Billy when the unfortunate accident occurred and had to pull over to the side of the road as they found it too difficult to continue riding while being convulsed with laughter. With tears streaming down their faces, they laughed until their sides ached. When they finally regained control of themselves, the boys were out of sight and Max and Steve had to sprint to catch up with the troop.

On his first campout, Billy was sleeping in a very small surplus army tent. He was a sound sleeper. When the troop bugler sounded reveille in the morning, Billy, apparently thinking that he was in the army, jumped out of his sleeping bag and assumed a modified position of attention. With tent poles and ropes hanging from his head, Billy stood in the hole he had ripped in the tent and with a lopsided grin on his face, wondered how he got where he was. Since he now had two entrances to his tent, Billy was pleased with the result. It only took him two weeks to fix the damage.

As he was learning to use the compass, Billy followed a compass course that Max had set up in the woods. He knew about compass bearings and he knew about pacing, but Billy seemed unable to do them simultaneously. As a result he often ended up several hundred yards from the intended completion point on a mile-long compass course. After his third attempt at following the course, Billy sadly wandered over to report to Max.

"How did you do this time, Billy?" questioned Max. "I see you ended up in the right county."

"I don't know, Max. I keep getting farther away from the destination. We must be in the middle of a magnetic storm and its fouling up my compass," offered a bewildered Billy with his original explanation for compass malfunction.

In the darkness, Steve realized that Billy had done it again. Standing in his soaking wet tennis shoes, Billy told Steve that his feet were starting to get cold.

"I thought you had a pair of boots to wear on the campout, Billy," Steve observed dryly.

"I couldn't find 'em," Billy said, his teeth rattling together like a machine gun. "Besides, the snow's melted at my house. I thought it was springtime."

With a "why me" glance toward the heavens, Steve told Billy to get his shoes off, dry his feet, put on some dry socks and underwear, and crawl in his sleeping bag.

"Dry socks?" whimpered Billy. "Was I supposed to bring dry socks?"

"Don't you remember our last troop meeting?" began Steve. "Oh, never mind! I'll get you a pair of socks."

After getting Billy tucked snugly, if not warmly, in his sleeping bag, Steve built a fire to dry out Billy's shoes. "We've got a problem, Max," Steve said, as his scoutmaster joined him at the fire.

"What did Billy do now?" Max asked innocently, a twinkle in his eye.

Steve explained the tennis-shoe problem and briefly

described the paltry contents of Billy's pack. "Don't these guys ever learn?" pleaded Steve.

"What do you suggest?" countered Max. "I don't want to leave early. This will be a fun campout."

"I guess Billy can sit around the fire tomorrow. We can give him some logs to prop up his feet with, so they stay out of the snow. He can't possibly get into trouble doing that. But he will miss the fun of gathering sap from the maple trees," Steve pointed out.

And so it happened. After breakfast the next day, Steve bored holes in several maple trees, inserted the spouts that funneled the sap outwards, and hung a collecting bucket from each spout. There were six buckets hanging on pegs. Hopefully, enough sap would be collected to boil down for maple syrup.

When Steve returned to camp, he found Billy sitting by the fire. Billy had thrown some wood on the fire that seriously dampened the heat but added significantly to the output of smoke. Of course, Billy was sitting downwind from the fire and smoke billowed around him, hiding him from view. A plaintive cry emanated from the shroud of smoke. "I hate smoke!"

Steve told Billy to move so he wasn't always sitting in the smoke.

"I have," Billy replied. "A hundred times. Each time I do, the wind changes directions."

"Ah Billy, you're having one of those days, aren't you? Try using dry wood and the smoke isn't nearly as bad," Steve suggested airily.

"Dry wood? You use dry wood for fires?" queried Billy incredulously. "How do you find dry wood in the snow?"

Steve pulled out a large pot from his sack. Using some rocks he found nearby, Steve built a stand for the pot near the edge of the campfire. By early afternoon, Max decided enough sap had collected in the buckets to make a collection. With his scouts following him, Max made rounds of the tapped trees and collected about a gallon of sap.

"Okay, fellas, the idea is to heat the sap to near boiling so the water is evaporated. Removing all of the moisture will make maple sugar. Otherwise we will make the maple syrup for pancakes tomorrow. Keep stirring it so it doesn't stick to the bottom of the pot," counselled Max. "I'm going on a Second Class hike with a few of the boys."

Steve tried to keep an eye on the boiling sap. He stirred until he got tired, then turned the spoon over to Billy, who was sitting by the fire anyway. "Keep stirring, Billy. I've got to check on the other scouts."

When Max returned from the hike, he found Billy sitting in a pall of smoke, gasping for air, tears streaking down both cheeks, leaving rivulets of mud to mark their passage. His feet were soaked again and his pants were wet up to his knees. He was miserable.

"Billy, what happened?" Max asked, not really wanting to hear the answer.

"Steve left me to stir the sap," said Billy sobbing, pointing to a blackened mass of sludge congealed in the bottom of the sap pot. "But I lost the spoon."

"How did you stir it, Billy?" queried Max. "Did you use a stick?"

Dumbly nodding his head, Billy said that he had gone to his tent to get his mittens. It took awhile to find them and when he got back to the fire, the spoon was gone.

"I looked everywhere, Max," he said. "But I couldn't find it."

"Wait a minute Billy. Wasn't it a plastic spoon?" asked Max. "A black plastic spoon?"

"I think so, Max," responded Billy. "Do you know where it went?"

Max picked up Billy's stirring stick and fished around in the bottom of the sap pot. He snagged something that felt a little thicker than maple syrup should and gingerly lifted it out. It slipped off the stick and plopped back into the pot where it oozed back into the brew. Again Max fished the blob out and held it up for inspection.

"Here's your spoon, Billy. I didn't want maple syrup on my pancakes, anyway."

Boardman Winter

Dave and Steve left school early Friday afternoon headed for the banks of the Boardman River where the troop was going to spend a late winter weekend camping in the still-deep snow. The rest of the troop was going to show up later in the day after Max got off from work and could collect the other boys.

They had an idea for a camp that seemed worth trying. Steve had found what appeared to be part of an old yellow-and-green striped canvas awning while rummaging around in the shed behind his house. It was four feet wide and thirty feet long. There were grommets every four feet along the edges and at each corner. Steve and Dave planned on using it to make a cozy winter camp.

Dave parked his mom's '57 Chevy station wagon as far off the road as he could without getting stuck. Like his scout uniforms, the Chevy was green and his mom sometimes let him think it was his car. Of course she trusted him to drive carefully. He was proud of his car. It had *three by the knee* and Dave could hit seventy in second gear without working her too hard. So far his mom didn't know about teenagers, Chevies, and 283's.

All of their equipment was tied to their pack boards using diamond hitches. It made a bulky load. Lashing on snowshoes before hoisting on their packs, Dave and Steve settled into a rhythm of walking with shoes four feet long. It was necessary to pick up one shoe far enough so that it crossed over the top of the other, while gracefully swinging the leg forward. If the first snowshoe wasn't elevated high enough, its edge caught the rawhide lashing on the edge of the other snowshoe bringing the wearer to a halt, usually face down in the snow. Which Steve immediately accomplished, doing a head plant in the snow after tripping on his own shoe.

Since Dave had kept going, anxious to find the perfect clump of cedar trees for their experiment, Steve was left with the tricky task of getting vertical on his own. His snow shoes were no longer flat on the snow. In fact they were perpendicular to the ground, with his knees touching in the middle. He fumbled around, trying desperately to find something hard against which he could push, but Steve was out of luck. There wasn't even a nearby tree to hold for assistance. Finally, frustration winning the battle, Steve shrugged off his pack before unlacing one of his snowshoe bindings. He then was able to sit on his still attached snowshoe and reattach his other one. Grunting back into his pack, Steve set out, following Dave's trail.

Ten minutes later he caught up with Dave who was standing, hands on hips, surveying a clump of cedar trees that grew near the bank of the deep dark river.

"Didja have a nice hike in here, Steve?" asked Dave smirking. "Sorry I couldn't stop to help you. I figured you needed some practice with the big shoes."

"Right. Thanks," responded Steve, "Does this look like what we need?"

"It sure does. Let's get out our saws," Dave said excitedly. "We want to be really comfortable when Max shows up."

Both boys took off their packs and set them carefully on their snow shoes. Each located his folding saw and both boys stamped around under the cedar trees, packing the snow down solidly. When they had a firm surface for working, each boy started sawing off the interior branches of the cedar trees to a height of six feet. All of the branches were carefully piled on one side of the clearing to keep them from getting wet.

Their next project was to build a sleeping platform two feet off the ground big enough to hold two sleeping bags. They used diagonal and square lashings to assemble the four vertical posts and the outside edges of the platform. Across the entire structure, Dave and Steve laid dead branches they had gathered along the river. On top of the dead branches, the cedar boughs that they had trimmed were stacked, making a thick comfortable mattress.

From his pack Steve retrieved his hideously colored awning and dragged it back into the hollowed-out clump of cedar trees. Dave dropped his hatchet when he saw what Steve had dredged out of his pack.

"Where on earth did you get that?" Dave asked, astonishment etched on his face. "Do you really expect me to sleep with that thing near me? The noise of its colors will keep me awake all night!"

"Come on, Dave. I did the best I could. Besides, you can't see it in the dark."

"We'll be easy to find if someone comes looking for us. Max won't even have to follow our tracks. He can just listen for the sound," retorted Dave.

The buddies stretched the awning around the interior of the cedar clump. With the convenient grommets, they tied it to the trees so that it made a full circle inside the cedars, overlapping, but extending beyond the end of the sleeping platform so that it formed a door that blocked any vagrant river breezes. From the edge of the bed to the far wall was a distance of about eight feet. Near the far wall, Dave began laying rocks that he had dredged up from the unfrozen river bank, forming a neat fire ring. Behind the ring, Steve constructed a wall of short cedar logs, making a reflector for Dave's fire.

Since they had left all of the outside cedar limbs on the trees, except for the doorway, Dave and Steve were pretty secure in their weekend structure. Not much wind penetrated through to the interior, so smoke could rise straight up through the chimney of cedar boughs. It was a decent setup and took them about three hours to complete.

Max and the rest of the troop showed up after dark. By then, Steve and Dave were cooking tinfoil dinners on their reflector oven. When Max stuck his head in the doorway, the outside temperature was about twenty degrees. Steve and

Dave were sitting on their sleeping platform in their shirt sleeves sipping hot chocolate. It was fifty degrees in their riverbank hideaway.

"Hi, Max," welcomed Dave. "You want some hot chocolate?"

"You guys," muttered Max, as he backed out to see if he could find a good camping place in the dark. Fortunately it was too dark for Max to get a good look at the set up in Dave and Steve's camp.

After eating a hasty tinfoil dinner, Dave and Steve got dressed and went out to help the younger, less fortunate scouts prepare for a robust night of camping.

They helped excavate snow holes so the rest of the troop could pitch their tents on the ground, then helped them set up the tents. They helped gather firewood in the dark and showed them how to find dry bark in the winter so fires could be started easier. Steve and Dave showed the younger scouts how a good reflector fire can be useful in keeping warm.

As he watched his older scouts teaching the younger boys, Max felt really positive about what was happening in his troop. In spite of his misgivings, Max realized that he had a pretty good bunch of boys. They were willing to help each other. In fact they seemed to try to make sure the needs of other scouts were met before taking care of themselves. Even on a cold winter camp with snow everywhere, service was really important.

On Saturday, when Max got up to make his first cup of morning coffee, he looked over towards the clump of cedars where Steve and Dave were hibernating. Even though it was only a hundred feet away, Max could barely make out the doorway that was facing directly towards him. Beyond the doorway was a faint glow that Max couldn't explain. Sipping his coffee with his hands around the cup for warmth, Max wondered what could possibly be shining in the early morning light since the sun wasn't yet above the tree tops.

Curiosity finally overwhelmed him and Max donned his boots and jacket and headed over to see Dave, his senior patrol leader. Sticking his head around the corner of the doorway,

Max was startled to see the awful awning stretched around the cedar trees. Dave and Steve were blissfully unaware of the presence of their visitor, since both were still slumbering in their sacks on top of their cedar bed. "My gosh," Max exclaimed! "This looks like the coat of many colors Joseph wore in the Bible. Is one of you guys for sale?"

"Oh hi, Max," said Dave yawning, "It's pretty awful, isn't it? But it sure is warm. Come on in and sit a spell. Steve's going to get up and light the fire. Aren't you, Steve?"

"No way, Dave. It's your turn," Steve replied sleepily, just as Dave's foot propelled him off the platform to land in a heap near Max's feet.

"Good morning, Max," said Steve as he scrambled out of his sleeping bag. "I guess it's my turn to build the fire. Say, do you like our setup?"

"I think," said Max, as he turned on his heel to return to his tent, "that it is probably the worst-looking shelter I have ever seen in my life. It's a good thing you chose to hide it in the bushes. Can I come over for breakfast?"

Steve's Eagle

It had been five years before when Steve sat in The Bowl at scout camp, watching his first outdoor court of honor. Max had presented Steve with his Tenderfoot award that night, pinning it on upside down, following troop tradition. Steve had pinned the miniature Tenderfoot badge on his mother's tan dress while his father looked on. Later in the evening, as the campfire faded and the stars became visible, Max had presented the Eagle award to Jim, who was senior patrol leader. Jim was sixteen years old and stood tall that night, firelight glinting from his glasses. Steve was just eleven. But Steve promised himself that he would, someday, be an Eagle scout like Jim.

Now it was Steve's turn. Over the years he had worked diligently on advancement and then earning merit badges for the higher ranks. He had attended summer camp for three years, earning two merit badges each summer. During his first year in high school, Steve had been on camp staff, working in the kitchen as a dishwasher. During that summer he had earned a few more merit badges. For most of his required merit badges, though, Steve had to contact a merit badge counselor and set up an initial appointment at which he would find out the expectations of the counselor.

He found out most often, that the counselor expected Steve to learn the material, then set up an appointment to discuss what he had learned. The counselor always asked pointed questions that helped Steve focus on important issues in the topic under study. Then they would set a date for a future meeting to discuss more discoveries. Often Steve had six or seven meetings with a counselor before it was determined that

Steve knew enough to demonstrate proficiency in a particular merit badge. When Steve was a senior in high school, he finally completed the requirements for his Eagle award.

Members of his board of review included, Max, his scoutmaster, Bob, a scoutmaster from another troop, and Joe, a longtime scouter representing the council. Between them, the board members represented over seventy-five years of scouting. Steve's board of review had lasted for three hours. During that time he had explained the requirements for each merit badge that he had earned and demonstrated that he still retained a working knowledge of each subject. He explained how important scouting was to him, how he tried each day to live up to his responsibilities as a member of Troop 35 and the Boy Scouts of America. Because of his nervousness after completing the board of review, Steve was relieved to find out, following an hour's deliberation, that he had passed the board of review. He had been examined by three scouts he respected greatly, each of whom wore an Eagle knot on his uniform, and been found worthy to also wear the Eagle badge.

As part of the regular troop court of honor that September, Steve was presented with his Eagle badge in the lodge at scout camp. It had been built recently to replace the previous one that had burned down. So Steve was completing the process that had begun five summers before when he promised himself that he would be an Eagle scout like Jim: he was closing the circle.

Steve told Max that he would be honored if Max would present his Eagle award to him. Max had over six hundred boys through his troop by then. Some of them had stayed for only a few months. Most had been around for several years. A relatively few became Eagle scouts. All of them thought that Max was probably the greatest influence in their lives outside of their families. Steve certainly felt that way. His dad travelled a lot, getting home only a couple of weekends each month, and Steve loved and respected him as a friend and father. But much of Steve's character had been shaped by Max, who taught by example, the important lessons of life.

In the lodge, huge windows looked over the pine trees above the lake where the camp waterfront was located. Because of the darkness outside, the windows reflected the Eagle ceremony back to the audience. As Steve stood before the assembled families of Troop 35, he looked into his scoutmaster's eyes, noting the twinkle that was perpetually evident when Max was having fun. Watching Max, Steve realized that happiness cannot be shown in a smile without also appearing in the eyes. Looking at the reflection in the glass, Steve could see his parents standing behind him. His mom was wearing the same tan dress she had worn at the court of honor those five long years ago when he had become a Tenderfoot scout. With pride she wore all five of her advancement pins on her left lapel. They had come a long way together, Steve and his mom: Steve learning about life through scouting and merit badges, Mom driving him to meet with counselors, sharing what he had learned as they travelled the roads of scouting together. He imagined that he could see the same twinkle in their eyes. He knew it was there. For the first time, while looking in the reflection, Steve also realized that he was as tall as his father; he had grown to the stature of a man.

At the conclusion of the ceremony, Steve took Max's left hand firmly in his hand saying, "Thanks, Max. I couldn't have done it without you." The twinkle was still there in Max's eyes, but it was accented by two glistening streaks descending vertically down his cheeks.

Turning to his parents, Steve felt a man's handshake from his father, who was not a hugging man. His dad's twinkling eyes formed the bottom of an inverted exclamation point: tears of pride were apparent also on his dad's cheeks. The hug from mom was anti-climactic: she had probably done as much as Steve had to earn the Eagle award, but the recognition went to her son that night. Forever after, though, she wore her Eagle pin as proudly as Steve.

67

Summer Camp

Of course, the area assigned to the troop was the farthest from the parking lot, which meant a carry of a half-mile with all of the camping gear needed for a week. Each patrol had a huge box, which contained all of the accumulated kitchen equipment that the boys decided they needed during the week. Most of it would be unused. A stack of lashing poles was also necessary for constructing camp gates, axe yard areas, flag poles, and patrol projects. A small semi-trailer would have been more appropriate for hauling them than on the top of Max's truck. Many of the lashing poles would also be unused. The boys did not remember from one summer camp to the next what equipment was really necessary.

Max, with some assistant scoutmasters, had taken the boys to summer camp deep in the northern forests. It was early in the year and the boys were the first group of the summer to use the remote camping place. They were a day early. Max liked to use the full week of summer camp for scouting activities, not have to use part of the first day to set up camp when the boys could be working on advancement.

Some camp staff members showed up near dinnertime. By then most of the camp was in order. Pierre had assigned the patrols to various secluded corners of the large troop area. All of the tents were pitched according to Pierre's unerring eye for neatness and order. A large screened dining area had been erected in the center of camp near the scoutmasters' tents so the Green Bar group could meet when needed. Chuck, one of the assistant scoutmasters, had laboriously supervised the other scoutmasters in erecting his tepee so that the entrance

68

faced the rising sun. Streamers fluttered gracefully from the many poles of the tepee that were describing a small circle high above the camp.

The patrols were working together on dinner preparation, and the scoutmasters were sitting in the screened dining area talking about the plans for the week. The camp staffers were curious. No other troops came to scout camp a day early. None of the other troops would arrive with five members in the scout-master corps. None of the others would bring an enormous tepee to set up in the center of camp. None of the other troops would be singing scout songs as they fixed dinner.

"Hello, the camp," called one of the staffers. "Is it okay if we come into your camp area?"

"Welcome," called back Max. To the other scoutmasters, he said, "At least they understand some camp etiquette and asked permission to come in."

Being an old collector of scouting memorabilia, Chuck asked if any of the staffers traded patches. A couple of the guests responded affirmatively, so Chuck realized he was in for a good week. Scouting adventures were pleasantly exchanged for a quarter hour or so until the patrols announced that dinner was ready by giving their patrol yells. Max invited the staffers to have dinner with them, but the offer was politely declined.

"Thanks," said one staffer. "We've already eaten. Can we come back during the week?"

"Sure," responded Chuck. "Remember to bring your patches!"

"You bet," came the reply. "Oh. By the way. There's a rumor that a bear has been seen in the area. Enjoy your dinner."

After dinner was eaten and the cooking mess was beaten into partial submission, the troop gathered around the fire in the Beaver patrol camping area. Max entertained the assembled scouts with Robert Service's "The Cremation of Sam McGee." Skits were presented spontaneously by groups of boys. The groans from those viewing were in direct proportion to the vintage of the skit. There seemed to be no such thing as an original skit. As the blaze dwindled, the camp staffers again hailed the camp and asked to join the campfire.

Wishing to impress the boys in the troop with their scout spirit, the staffers asked to lead a couple of songs they were sure the scouts had never heard before. With each song, the boys in the troop said, "We just did that one. What have you got that is new?"

Realizing that Max's troop was really top notch in singing and campfires, the staffers settled in to enjoy the smell of the campfire and the scent of the forest. As the campfire faded and the songs turned quiet, a shuffling could be heard in the brush some distance above camp. Then silence descended over the group. Only the popping of wood on the dying campfire disturbed the calm.

"What was that?" whispered Curt. Before Chuck could respond to his son's question, one of the staffers repeated the rumor of the bear in camp. It seemed like a typical ghost story told by older boys for the benefit of the younger in the shank of the evening around a dying campfire.

"Oh. It's just an old porcupine. Nothing to worry about," offered Max. "Pierre, let's wrap up this campfire. Tomorrow's a big day."

"Troop dis . . ." whispered Pierre.

"Missed," whispered back the boys.

As he walked back toward the Flaming Arrow camp, Curt sidled up to his dad and inquired, "Are there really bears around here?"

"Naw," replied Chuck. "They're just trying to scare you. It happens every summer. See you in the morning."

A half-hour later, Curt crawled under the flap of the tepee, dragging his pillow and sleeping bag through the dirt with him.

Very patiently, Chuck stumbled off from his cot, slipped into his scout shorts and moccasins and, taking the bag and pillow from Curt, walked up the hill with him, returning to the patrol campsite.

"You'll be fine, Curt. There really is nothing to be afraid of."

Early the next morning, Max and his boys went to the waterfront to do a swimming check. Every one had his buddy tag filled out and it only needed to be colored to indicate the owner's swimming ability. Billy was talking non-stop. In spite of the cool air, he was perspiring profusely. As the scouts gathered along the dock, the waterfront director told them that they needed to enter the water and swim three laps between the buoys if they wanted to have full waterfront privileges. To Max, Billy seemed really nervous. Billy balanced on one leg as he dipped the big toe on his other foot into the bracing water of the northern lake. As he did so, Billy shivered twice and looked like he was about to have a tooth removed without anesthesia.

"Jump in," came the command. Fifteen bodies exploded from the dock in various postures from very graceful to the wounded-duck bellyflop of Billy, who hit the water and immediately sank out of sight. *Gee, I hope he can swim,* thought Max. Within two very rapid heartbeats, Billy burst from the water and landed back on the dock, almost as if a projectionist had reversed the film of Billy's diving attempt. With teeth clanking together and lips blue, Billy hugged his chest for warmth and told Max that he would try the swim check later if that was all right, thank you just the same.

While the rest of the troop finished the swim check, Billy warmed himself in the morning sun. Since he was already dry by the time the others were back on the beach, Billy dressed and began the hike back to camp alone. The rest of the troop was a few minutes behind him. With Max in the lead, they had just crossed a small stream, when wild-eyed Billy came racing down the trail screaming, only semi-coherently, that there was a bear in the camp.

"Calm down," counseled Max. "Think about it for a minute and then tell us what you think you saw."

Rushing on, in spite of Max's request, Billy told of seeing a black head moving through the bushes near the base of the

71

hill where the Flaming Arrow patrol was camped.

"It had a long nose, black eyes, and pointy ears," Billy said. "I know it was a bear."

"Show us where," ordered Chuck.

Billy led the rest of the troop to an area near a stand of blackberry bushes and pointed.

"He was over there. This is as close as I'm going," announced Billy.

"Wait here," was Chuck's response. "I used to study bears."

He cautiously walked to the bushes and peered under them, carefully examining the ground. He straightened up and sniffed the wind, rotating slowly as he did so. Then he began to examine the ground in ever-widening circles, looking for bear tracks. After a ten-minute search, Chuck rejoined the troop, telling them that, in his opinion there had not been a bear in the area. Billy was just letting his imagination run wild.

"There were no tracks," said Chuck. "And you can smell a bear. There was no odor either."

"Let's get cleaned up," suggested Max. "We have a lot of advancement to do this week." With that the boys scattered to their patrol areas.

As the scoutmasters gathered in the dining area, Max asked the others if it was possible for a bear to be in the area.

"Possible but not likely," offered Chuck, sagaciously. "They usually won't come this close to people."

Later in the day, during the heat of the afternoon, Max was strolling back to camp. He had been out checking on the boys, making sure they were getting all of their classes in and not spending all of their time and money the first day of camp at the trading post. Pierre seemed to have things under control. The boys were all busy. Max decided it would be a good time to think about the rest of the week and what needed to be done. On hot afternoons, Max usually found such thinking was best done with his eyes closed while in a supine position.

As he entered the camp, Max noticed Chuck walking up the trail towards the Flaming Arrow campsite. Walking stick in hand, Chuck seemed to be checking on the tidiness of the campsites. Suddenly, Chuck's walking stick flew into the air, cartwheeling in slow motion, sunlight flashing from its polished surface. It reached the top of its skyward arc within twenty feet. In that amount of time, Chuck spun around, throwing up clouds of dust with his spinning feet before gaining the needed traction, and accelerated past a dining fly and close enough to the troop flag that the suction created by his rapid passage unfurled the flag as if it was blowing in a strong breeze before skidding to a wobbly halt next to Max. His eyes were wide with wonder.

"Bear. It's a bear."

"Slow down, Chuck. What's going on?"

"It was coming out of Curt's tent," said Chuck. "The kids must have left some food in the tent."

"Let's go see," countered Max, as he headed up the hill, pausing long enough to retrieve Chuck's walking stick. "You might need this," he said, handing back the carved work of art.

The bear was ambling down the far side of the hill when Max reached the top of the Flaming Arrow hill. He seemed totally unconcerned about his recent precipitous encounter with Chuck. In fact, he acted as if seeing a wild man with a bushy red mustache was a common occurrence. Even one who had such a hard time holding on to his hiking stick.

As the boys straggled back to camp, they gathered by the dining fly and listened as Max described Chuck's encounter with the nonexistent bear. With each telling, the story took on more intense details until the only parts resembling the truth were that Chuck had seen a bear and Max had witnessed the discovery. The rest was pure fabrication.

For the rest of the week, the bear was a frequent visitor in the scouts' camp. Except for one near panic-stricken incident when Billy ran down to the headquarters of camp, shouting that a bear had attacked Chuck in camp, and the camp staffers had appeared in camp on a rescue mission armed with bows and target arrows to save the scouts in Troop 35, everything was fine. The bear didn't seem to mind sharing the woods with the scouts. And the scouts got used to having a bear in camp. Except for Curt, who spent the week sleeping under a cot in a tepee despite his father's assurances that the bear would not cause problems.

Pierre's Departure

Pierre was sitting at the table with the rest of the Green Bar leaders when Roy came into the gym where the scout meeting was being held. He had been gone for a while, recalled Roy, *He looks different,* Roy thought. *Much more intense.* Pierre had on his scout uniform that night. His campaign hat was still curled up fore and aft with the first class pin on the front of it. His Star award was still pinned to the left pocket of his shirt, which seemed to fit just a little too snugly. All five of his merit badges were still in place on his right shirt sleeve. The hem of his scout pants had been let out a few times but still nicely covered his worn, leather boots. *It's something about the eyes,* thought Roy as he remembered the trails and rivers they had travelled together. *He must be about nineteen now,* he mused, deciding that it had been at least six months since he last saw Pierre.

After the opening ceremony, Max introduced Pierre to the troop.

"This is Pierre, the scout you have all heard about," said Max and then he paused, allowing the nervous laughter to subside. "He thought it would be a good idea to go on a hike tonight. Pierre is in the Army," Max continued. "He just got home from boot camp."

Without further ado, Pierre lined up the scouts by patrol and headed out of the back door of the gym, across the playground, and through the fence heading for a bare hill to the west, which rose above the forest like an abscessed tooth. He didn't pause to look back. He assumed the scouts would follow him just as they always did. Of course he was right.

Reaching the base of the tortured hillside, Pierre scrambled up a steep clay cliff until he came to a shoe-width ledge that traversed the exposed escarpment, before disappearing into the brush on either end. It was fifty feet above the trail the scouts had followed to reach the hillside. Upon reaching the ledge, Pierre flattened himself against the face of the cliff and began inching his way along it, slowing extending his left foot, testing the strength of the ledge with his weight, before following with his right foot. Roy was still at the bottom of the cliff, and he paused to watch Pierre perform his balancing act.

Although Roy lived within a mile of the hill, he had never tried climbing the cliff before and the thought of doing so now was less than appealing. Roy let the other two patrols ascend the precipitous clay bank before leading his patrol up its face. By then Pierre had disappeared into the brush and was, judging from the noise, heading for the hilltop.

As Roy began his ascent, he thought of some of the things he had learned previously while hiking with Pierre. First, he had developed a keen sense of direction coupled with steadiness in reading a map. Both skills had been necessary in finding the way back after Pierre had unerringly gotten the scouts lost on previous hikes. Roy now understood that, though a person might become fatigued, there were, almost always, energy reserves that could be tapped to carry on a toilsome journey. It was always possible to take one more step. He also understood the importance of setting a good example in every aspect of scouting, from wearing a complete uniform and proper foot gear to showing scout spirit with patrol yells, songs, and corny skits. He understood the importance of steady and regular advancement through the ranks.

After climbing only a few steps, Roy realized that Pierre was, again, teaching him something that he needed to learn for himself. Most things when tried, are not as bad or as difficult as they once seemed. Nothing is ever as hard or as scary as one thought. Though he had never climbed like this before, Roy found that he actually enjoyed it. When he reached the narrow ledge and began moving across it, he noticed that, as long as he didn't look down for too long, it wasn't much different than trying to walk along a railroad track without losing his balance. Just a little farther off the ground.

Roy carefully led his patrol off the ledge, making sure that his younger scouts were succeeding in this new challenge. The sun was dancing on the western horizon when Roy reached the summit and began the descent of the north face. When Roy's patrol reached a gravel road, Pierre was at the edge of the road down on his hands and knees looking into the opening of a twenty-four inch culvert that crossed under the road. With a *follow me* look on his face, Pierre entered the culvert, and began crawling towards the far end. Keeping an interval of ten feet, the rest of the scouts entered the tunnel and crawled along, knees painfully abraded by the corrugations of the metal and shoulders scraping the top.

Overcoming his reticence at entering dark confined spaces, Roy closed his eyes and entered the tunnel's breech. The tunnel was only fifty feet in length but seemed longer. Apparently there was a substantial drop to the ground below the end of the culvert, and it was easiest to exit while lying on your back. That enabled you to grab the top edge of the culvert prior to pulling your feet out, hanging on the edge and then dropping to the ground. After an interminable passage, Roy opened his eyes in time to see, Tom, the scout in front of him, begin to turn around in the culvert. In doing so Tom became stuck: a human barricade, unable to either advance or retreat.

Overcoming his momentary panic, Roy decided the best way out was to help Tom from his predicament. Tugging gently on Tom's pant leg, Roy talked him through the process of becoming mobile once more. *He did it to me again,* screamed Roy silently to himself, as he realized that Pierre had created another imbroglio for the scouts but, in doing so, helped them grow by having to solve a Gordian knot.

When Roy crawled out of the culvert, he looked towards the west. The sun had descended below the horizon and was invisible. Cloud tops were on fire: the pinks, oranges, and reds of a cool citrus drink. Roy realized that the sun was also setting on the career of a boy scout. Pierre would never again lead

77

the troop on a hike as a boy. His days of camping with the troop were probably over. Sometimes Pierre had been overbearing when dealing with other scouts, but that was only when an activity was being experienced. Later, in the calm reflection of memory, *Pierre hikes* really seemed fun, something to be endured in reality but bragged about in hindsight.

For Roy, the hike back to where Max patiently waited was poignant. He knew, for the first time, that boyhood was not a profession, merely a series of experiences that helped prepare a boy to face the responsibilities of manhood.

Roy knew that he was lucky. As an Eagle scout, he had more and better experiences than most scouts. When Roy's father had died, Max had helped fill that void in his life, being both a father and a friend as well as scoutmaster. What Max had taught Roy would be a great help in facing the imponderables of life.

Back in the gym, Pierre thanked the scouts for going on one last hike with him. Around the electric campfire set up in the middle of the gym floor, he told of his experiences in boot camp. The hours were long and tedious. Drill instructors were not quite human in their demands of the recruits. He told of long runs with the other soldiers, packs on backs and rifles on shoulders, and the initial agony felt all over the body when muscles were asked to do unaccustomed tasks. He shared stories of push ups, marching, inspections, running, short haircuts, angry voices, bugles, rifles, close-order drill, gunfire, letters from home, and fatigue. He told of the importance of teamwork and dependability in formidable situations. Then Pierre told of the pride that comes at the completion of a difficult task. And the camaraderie that comes with people who share those tasks.

Pierre met and momentarily kept the gaze of each scout around the fire. "I know you guys think I have been a jerk over the years. I guess sometimes maybe I have. I won't apologize for that. That's the way I am. You need to know that the things Max has been teaching you about life are crucial."

As Pierre talked, Roy recognized that what he had learned

from Max had kind of crept up on him, like dew on the morning grass. You don't see it form, but in the morning it is there, gleaming in the early sun. He knew that there comes a point in a boy's life when he must put away the things of a boy. That bit of knowledge explained the difference in Pierre's eyes. He *had* seen things that boys weren't meant to see and because he had done so could not go back to being a boy. Like Hannibal, Pierre had crossed the Rubicon into adulthood.

Intrigued by his discovery, Roy knew, for the first time, that in two short years he would put youthful things behind him and go about the business of life as an adult. Boyhood was the training ground for manhood, and, since the death of his own father, Max had become his teacher. With clarity Roy saw his career in the military, knowing that he would be a leader of men.

Max's Philosophy

One night, Max and Barry were in Max's den drinking coffee and talking about the troop. Barry had been one of Max's assistants for a lot of years. Together they had worked with a lot of boys, helping them with advancement, hiking and camping with them, being their friends. Only with a great effort were they able to contain the inner mirth that they shared as they remembered some of the more outrageous escapades some of their scouts had been involved in. It was fun, that sharing of good times together. It was the kind of evening all old scouts experience when reminiscing around a campfire, friendship as warm as the coffee.

The awareness that some of their former scouts had passed away brought some sadness with the realization that they would no longer be able to share trails together. The somber tones were cast quickly aside when Max and Barry reflected on all of the growth the departed scouts had made in their young lives. "We were fortunate to have shared a small slice of their lives," both agreed.

"If scouting has been so good to us, Max, why don't we affect the lives of more boys?" Barry questioned.

"I don't know, Barry. I guess scouting is for all boys, but all boys aren't for scouting. We both know how much good can come in a boy's life when he experiences a good scouting program. I had a great experience as a scout. I know you did, too. I owe a tremendous debt to scouting, the payback for a boyhood of treasured memories. Maybe there aren't enough leaders with good memories like us," responded Max thoughtfully.

"If that's the case, if scouting is a good program for boys, why can't we get parents to help us, Max?" queried Barry. "It seems like they are interested in having their kids in a good scouting program but are unwilling to help us. Sometimes it seems like they dump off their kids, saying, 'here, you take 'em, bring 'em home when you're done.'"

"That may be true, Barry. Do you remember parents helping in your troop when you were a boy?"

"Now that you mention it, I don't. The lack of support still bothers me. Sometimes I think we should tell the parents that we don't want their boys in the troop unless we get some parent support," groused Barry. "Besides, some of the boys don't seem to be really interested in scouting. Especially if it involves work."

"Come on, Barry. Why punish the boys because of their parents? The troop is made up of, as it always has been, really great boys, learning the way boys do, and at the speed that most boys do, with some adults as leaders who are close friends, following them around so that they can relive the childhood activities that they don't want to lose or forget. The boys aren't perfect, and it makes me really glad that they aren't. If we didn't need to work with them, train them, teach them, gently direct or guide them, and love them, we wouldn't have anything to do."

"But, Max, I get tired of always carrying the ball. Sometimes I think I need a break from scouting," continued Barry. "I usually spend two or three weekends a month doing scout stuff. Besides, some of the boys aren't too responsible."

"I have come to realize," said Max with feeling coming from deep within, "that a lot of what occurs at scout meetings does not affect me in the same way it does the *normal* population. I can see some of the dumbest stunts, unacceptable performances, and absolute foolishness of boys and think it is great. I really get a kick out of them whether they have spread camping gear all over my yard and left most of it out or something else equally dumb. I love those boys and I am just plain tickled to be with them, even under trying times, and I am grateful for every dumb thing they do. Every minute with the troop is a joy to me, whether I realize it then or if it takes a little time to find the joy in the event. Sometimes they can't start a fire or even raise a flag without goofing up, and it is just fine. When they do that, maybe, just maybe, they are telling us that as long as they are boys, we will still be needed." Then, realizing that he had rambled on, carried away with the memories of boys who learn by doing, he cleared his throat as he looked for a handy bandanna with which to wipe his eyes.

Barry was embarrassed by the feelings that Max had shared, so he grabbed both cups and went out to the kitchen where Lil was just finishing a fresh pot of coffee.

"Hi, Barry. I didn't know you were here. Have some coffee. How are things with scouts?"

"I don't know, Lil, I guess I'm getting a little tired of spending so much time with such little support from families."

"Ahhh," said Lil, thoughtfully. "Scouting does require a tremendous commitment, doesn't it? You know Max told me yesterday that he was lucky to be a scout leader. He felt blessed by God for every minute he got to share with scouts. And he's gone a lot with them. Even when Max is not here, boys often drop by to talk for a while. It's as if they have no one else to share with."

"I don't know how the two of you do it, Lil. Right now I seem to have lost the joy of scouting. I'd better take these back. Thanks for the coffee," Barry said as he retreated towards the den.

"Here's a fresh cup for you, Max," announced Barry as he crossed the den, holding the cup in his extended hand.

"What?" said Max, returning to the room from far away. "Oh, thanks, Barry. I was thinking about all of my years in scouting. Did you know that the first time I ever saw a scout book was at my cousin's house? It was in a glass bookcase. My aunt saw me looking at it and asked if I wanted to read it. She told me to be careful with it, but I could read it whenever I came over to her house. It took about three months of visits before I was able to finish reading it from cover to cover."

"You never told me that, Max. Thanks for sharing it with

me," offered Barry lamely. "I'm sorry I dumped all of this on you. I guess I'd better be going. Thanks for your time tonight."

"Barry, when you look at the boys, remember the stars in the night sky. Focus on the sparkling lights up there and the exceptional shooting stars not on the darkness between the stars. That's what I try to do," noted Max as he wrapped his arm around Barry's shoulder. "I'm glad you're part of Troop 35."

Philmont

For many of the boys in the troop, these were the first mountains that they had ever viewed. As the sun stretched its rosy fingers westward across the morning sky, the scouts were nearing LaJunta, Colorado. In the dawn of the high plains, they could see incredible vistas out either side of the train. To the northwest, towering over nearby mountains and covered with a mantle of lingering snow, soared the mighty summit of Pike's Peak, showpiece of Colorado's front range and one of fifty-four mountains in Colorado rising over 14,000 feet. Because of the dense forests near their home in the north, scouts in Troop 35 were seldom able to see for more than a few miles. Max estimated that the purple-and-white summit of Pike's Peak was nearly a hundred miles away.

Max and his scouts were on their way to Philmont, the national Boy Scout ranch located near Cimarron, New Mexico. During the 1920s, Waite Phillips, of Phillips Petroleum fame, had donated a 137,000 acre ranch to the Boy Scouts of America with the only stipulations being that it continue to be a working cattle ranch and that the wilderness areas be preserved for use by Boy Scouts.

The mountains near Trinidad were passed slowly as the AT & SF train struggled up the grade towards the summit. Forest-covered canyons, pinnacles, and rugged crags held the interest of the scouts as the railway portion of their journey neared an end. Junipers, pinion pines, and the ubiquitous sagebrush were most predominant during the early trip up the grade. They gave way to aspens, spruces, and firs near the summit. Max was excited to have the opportunity to trek with his scouts at the legendary scout ranch. The trip by train gave the troop an opportunity to view parts of the country not normally seen by most people.

At Raton, New Mexico, the scouts disembarked from the train, retrieved their equipment sacks and backpacks, then boarded the buses for the final forty miles to Cimarron. In stark contrast to the mountain pass above Trinidad were the sagebrush flats along the road to Cimarron. To the northwest, the foothills of the Sangre de Cristos Mountains reared, north slopes covered with pines and firs. Antelope were abundant along the highway, their light brown hair set off by patches of white, with black horns curving outward from their ears. Their stiff-legged bounding made them look like the springboks seen by Baden-Powell during his years in Africa.

Cimarron was a dry sleepy town. Most businesses were located on a dirt road running parallel to the main highway. Others were on a modestly paved road to the north. The historical St. James Hotel was located to the south of town on the road to Philmont and boasted a fine dining area, spirits, and clean comfortable rooms. The scouts barely noticed the town. Two rapid blinks of the eye and the buses were through town headed over the last hills before reaching the scout ranch.

Surprising the scouts was a herd of buffalo that were grazing along the west side of the road. They looked just like the buffalo herd at home, only larger. The mountains were nearer now. The verdant ridges reminded Max of the mountains around the Ponderosa that Ben Cartwright had called home.

Passing the beautiful Villa Philmonte on the left, Max explained to the scouts that the Spanish-style mansion was the home of Waite Phillips. With the rest of Philmont, it was donated to the Boy Scouts and currently served as the home of the Volunteer Training Center, where adult leaders received training. Giving it hardly a glance, the scouts looked down the road to headquarters where they would begin their trek into the mountains.

Tent City. Accommodations for the night and 6,300 verti-

85

cal feet higher than the airport at home.

A physical recheck.

Blood pressure. "Fine."

Pulse. "A little high. Don't worry! You're at high altitude."

"Does everyone find it difficult to breathe at this elevation?"

"Not to worry. You'll get used to it . . . in about a week."

Meal tickets for the dining hall.

Waiting. Not very patiently.

"Is that the Tooth?"

Peaking above the upper ridge line west of camp loomed the Tooth of Time, a famous landmark on the old Santa Fe Trail. Nine thousand feet at the summit, its south face was a heart-stopping sheer vertical drop of a thousand feet.

Trading Post.

"What did I forget?"

"Gotta have a map."

"Look at those mountains! Ten thousand feet? Are we going to climb them?"

"Where's Baldy?"

"It's on this map, in the northern section."

"That's a long way. Are we going there?"

"Not this trip. We don't have time."

"Where do we start?"

"Zastrow."

"What's a Zastrow?"

"It's a camp. Here on the map."

"Uh-huh."

"Where do we end up?"

"Same place."

"And we're gone for a week?"

"Yep!"

"Wow!"

"Are there really bears here?"

"Right. You need a bear sack to store your food."

"What's a bear sack?"

"You put your things that have an odor in a sack and raise

it on a high tree limb at night."

"Why?"

"To keep bears from eating your food."

"Won't they eat me instead."

"Naw. You're a runt."

"Whew!"

"Line up here for pictures."

"The sun's too bright. I can't keep my eyes open."

"Close your eyes until I count to three, then open them. Remember to smile!"

"One. Two. Three."

Click. History.

"Smell that! What is it?"

"Sagebrush."

"Ahh!"

Dinner.

"I'm not hungry."

"Eat it. It may be your last good food for a week."

"O.K."

"It's too early to go to bed!"

"Max says it's time, so git."

"Good night!"

In the morning, following a hurried, little-remembered meal, Max and his scouts loaded their equipment on the bus and embarked on the last portion of their ride. The bus followed a narrow paved road south from headquarters until it reached Rayado, where it turned back to the west and followed a bumpy dirt road for three miles.

"Everyone off."

The ranger told the scouts that there were some rules that must be followed. Trail etiquette, he called them. "First, the trail is not wide enough for two groups to pass. Upbound groups have the right-of-way over downward groups. Second, any group with stock has the right of way over groups without stock. Step off the trail on the uphill side. Third, scouts never litter. Pack your trash out with you."

During the first day, Max and his scouts hiked through Juniper and Pinion forests. Keeping the Rayado Creek on their right, they began a slow ascent, heading for their first evening's campsite at Crags Camp. Starting gradually, as if allowing the scouts time to acclimatize, the trail passed Abreu and Old Abreu before swinging back to the south and going up quickly. Stopping every hour for a rest, the scouts were having a hard time breathing in the thin air of New Mexico. Squirrels were everywhere, looking and sounding like the red squirrels back home. The deer were different, though. They had giant ears and were darker in color.

"Mule deer," Max told them.

The Notch was nearly 8,200 feet in elevation after a climb of 1,300 feet in a little over three miles. The wind coming through the Notch was blowing about forty miles per hour. It quickly blew off Max's hat. It was retrieved by the Philmont ranger who was accompanying the troop.

"Bernoulli's Principle," noted the smiling ranger. "Notice how narrow the canyon is here? The narrow part decreases the air pressure, creating a vacuum that draws a rush of air from one side to the other. As pressure decreases, air speed increases. Here's your hat back."

The theory was less interesting than the view. Across the canyon were some spectacular crags that loomed from the side of Crater Peak and rose two hundred feet straight up. Near their feet, the rocks dropped steeply to the river, which rumbled down the canyon, sound lost in the distance. The Notch was a curious spot. Max felt the beginnings of vertigo and backed away from the edge of the trail.

"We have two kinds of rocks at Philmont," announced the ranger. "This one is a leverite," he noted, pointing to a large rock partially buried in the iron hard soil. "By comparison, this is a layerite," he said holding up a brilliant pink rock that glittered in the sun. "When you are finished looking at the big kind, you leverite there so some one else can see it later. When you are finished with a smaller rock," he said, indicating the quartz, "layerite back down for the next person. The only

88

things you should take from Philmont are memories and photographs. The only things you should leave are footprints."

After a brief lunch stop, the scouts hitched up their packs and continued the trek towards Crags Camp. Below the Crags that the scouts had seen from the Notch, the trail began a series of switchbacks that descended to the creek. A welcome change from slogging uphill for so long, the scouts were greatly enjoying this downhill portion until their ranger told them they would have to come up the same trail in the morning.

A hasty dinner was followed by a rush to get the bear sacks filled and on the cable strung between two trees before it got too dark to see. Tender feet were looked after, hot spots gently doused. The first day on the trail was a killer. Legs and backs ached from carrying heavy loads up steep trails. Taps was automatic shortly after sunset. Sleep came soon after.

Back on the trail by 9:00 A.M. on sore legs and feet. It took a half-mile before the scouts were warmed up and the kinks were gone. By then the scouts had reached the top of the switchback they had descended the previous day. It had been much easier going down.

The remainder of the morning hike was spent in a gradual three-mile descent to Fish Camp, where Max and his scouts had a leisurely lunch next to the junction of Rayado and Agua Fria Creeks. Just as they were ready to hoist their packs for the afternoon hike, a cowhand rode into camp, explaining that he was moving a small herd of cattle through the camp and up the trail.

"Ah'd be mighty obliged if ya'll would stand back from the bank jest a titch so's ya'll don't skeer ma critters," he drawled, looking every bit like the working cowboy he was.

Bellowing their displeasure, about twenty Herefords reluctantly splashed across the creek, heading upstream at the urging of the trio of cowhands on the cattle drive. Following soon after the herd up Agua Fria Creek, Max and the scouts stepped carefully up the trail, which criss-crossed the creek constantly, avoiding any fresh cow deposits that were seen in time. Passing Aqua Fria Camp, the scouts continued a scenic hike through the southwest corner of Philmont. With Apache Peak in front of them, the scouts began another vicious switchback ascent as the trail rose up in the direction of Lost Cabin Camp where they would spend their second night.

Later, the scouts were standing in a meadow at 9,200 feet, gazing in awe at the stars painted on the canopy of the evening sky. The Milky Way was clearly visible, a sight seldom seen in the glow of night lights in the city.

"Look at the second star from the end in the handle of Ursa Major, the Big Dipper," urged their ranger, as he shared with them the beauty of the mountain sky. "If you look closely, you can see a second, much smaller star very close to it. According to the stories, if an Indian could see the smaller star, he had eyesight worthy of a warrior."

The next morning, as they were loading their backpacks, four weasels popped out of a hole near a root in the center of camp and headed, single file, up the trail, furry sine waves that were oblivious to the presence of scouts. The tips of their tails were black, and the rest of their fur was reddish-brown. Max told the scouts that in the winter their tail tips remain black, but the remainder of the weasel turned brilliant white.

"They're called ermine in the winter," he said. "Only their noses, eyes, and the end of their tails are visible against a blanket of snow."

Hiking back along the trail of the previous day, the ranger led the scouts to Apache Springs Camp where water flowed from a tap that didn't need to be treated. Water without an iodine taste was a rare commodity, and the extra mile hiked to obtain some was a small price to pay for that privilege. From there the scouts crossed Bear Creek and avoided Bear Canyon Camp, heading generally northeast all day. Crossing a ridge at 9,500 feet, the scouts reached their highest elevation of the trip before descending to Porcupine Camp.

"We've been out for three days now," noted Max. "It's time to change clothes. Darrell, you change with Mike. Lee, you change with Rich. Walt, no one will change with you."

"Aw, Max," groaned the scouts in unison.

"Seriously, fellows, it's time to do some laundry. Remember to wash your clothes at least two hundred feet from a water source. Just think, tomorrow you get to take a shower."

Holding their pungent apparel at arm's length, the scouts began the onerous task of trying to salvage their underwear and socks. Their efforts were only modestly successful, and they spread their ravaged clothing on bushes to dry in the sun. The meadow took on the air of a gypsy camp.

"Hey, fellows, I've got a song for you," announced the ranger. "After each line I sing, you guys come in with 'a ding dong.'"

Boy Scouts don't wear no socks.	A ding dong!
I was there when they took 'em off.	A ding dong!
They threw 'em in their packs.	A ding dong!
Then their moms had heart attacks.	
A ding dong, dong, dong, dong	
A ding dong, dong, dong, dong	
A ding dong, dong, dong, dong	
A ding dong.	

Boy Scouts don't wear no socks.	A ding dong!
I was there when they took 'em off.	A ding dong!
They threw 'em in a garbage can.	A ding dong!
Killed three rats and a garbage man.	
A ding dong, dong, dong, dong	
A ding dong, dong, dong, dong	
A ding dong, dong, dong, dong	
A ding dong.	

The fourth day was a short hike heading southeast along Rayado Creek again until reaching Phillips Junction where the scouts took the trail northeast towards Beaubien Camp. Beaubien sported showers, a food resupply, trash dump, fresh water, horses, a mail drop, and a trading post with lots of candy. Arriving at Beaubien just after lunch, the scouts set up an early camp before heading for the showers that were heated by a wood stove. Unfortunately, the stove didn't work, so they had an invigorating cold shower, shivering in the high mountain air. After dressing in semi-clean uniforms, the scouts headed for the trading post where they made a serious attempt to deplete the inventory of anything sweet and/or wet.

Day five saw the scouts taking a half-day ride on horses kept in the corral at Beaubien. The wranglers saddled the horses, attempting to match the size of the scout with the temperament of the steed. In doing so, the wranglers were mostly unsuccessful.

The horse Max rode was an ugly hammerhead roan. It tried to bite him several times before he was even seated in the saddle. After getting into the saddle and holding on to the horn like a rocking chair, Max nudged the roan in the ribs and muttered, "Git." The plug tried to rub him off on the poles of the corral. Pulling back on the reins caused the horse to back up into the corral poles.

"Man, this is a cantankerous horse," shouted Max. "What's his name?"

"Pierre," responded a wrangler, with a straight face. "He's meaner than a French chef."

"Of course," groaned Max. The rest of his response was lost in a stiff breeze.

The survivors from the horse ride stumbled back to their tents for a respite, easing chapped legs and sore behinds gently to the ground, bemoaning their lot in life.

"I'd sooner crawl home than get back on my horse," drawled Greg, rubbing his sore legs before leaning back, interlocking his fingers behind his neck and promptly falling asleep.

"I come all the way to Philmont and get stuck with a four-legged sack of dogfood named Pierre," groused Max. "He follows me everywhere!"

Dinner that night was provided by the staff at Beaubien. Bar-b-qued buffalo, corn on the cob, cowboy beans, and Dutch oven biscuits, the best meal of their entire trip. The scouts thought it was great, spending two nights in the same campsite. Packing up each morning was getting to be a real chore.

Morning found the stiffness gone from young bodies. Not so with older ones. The scouts were anxious to be on their way. Max was ready for another rest day. Prodding them onward their ranger indicated hiking along Bonito Creek, a good time to loosen sore muscles and an easy day since most of the trip was downhill as the trail dropped four hundred feet in a little more than three miles.

Lower Bonito Camp was located almost due south of Trail Peak. It was near its 10,250-foot summit that a bomber crew had run out of sky during World War II and crashed. One of the other trails passed the crash site, but Max's troop would not get near it. According to the ranger, only scattered bits of aluminum remained twenty-five years after the accident.

On day six, the scouts ascended four hundred feet and crossed the south shoulder of Fowler Mesa. After a brief rest on the flat top, Max led his scouts east towards their final camp. At the edge of the mesa, the trail dropped off steeply as it followed a break in the old lava flow. In a quarter mile, the trail dropped two hundred feet. Scrambling down the steep, zigzagging trail, the scouts were quickly off the mesa and following a much gentler trail that led to Aguila Camp. The doc was right. After a week at altitude, the scouts were no longer short of breath while hiking.

They found a campsite that perched at the edge of the mountain, offering a spectacular view to the southwest. It was a fifth of a mile lower than Lower Bonito, their camp from the previous night. At their feet, the mountain dropped away and, in the distance, became the sagebrush plains common to much of New Mexico. Far-off reservoirs glittered in the afternoon sun, brilliant flat pearls dropped by a careless giant. Overhead, hawks worked the thermals above the rock face through which the scouts had descended, looking for unwary animals small enough to capture. Above the camp, spring water poured out of a pipe protruding from the mountainside and cascaded into a bathtub-sized cement basin, the waters of which held a potpourri of microscopic fauna.

As the sun set that last night, huge cumulus clouds rolled

93

in from the southwest. While the tops of the clouds were bathed in a soft pink light, the bottoms were an angry blue-gray, the color of summer storms. Into the meadow danced three deer, the largest, a buck with antlers in velvet. They browsed through the scouts' camp, elegant players on a vast wilderness stage, fearless in their well-rehearsed roles.

Lightning split the sky, giving a preternatural glow to clouds that were lit violently from within. Thunder rumbled through the darkness, echoing from distant canyon walls before reluctantly rolling away: a senile giant muttering to himself. A gentle breeze massaged the treetops, whispering as it passed, heading towards Urraca Mesa. No rain fell to the ground. Like many summer storms in dry western climates, clouds rolled in, the wind blew, and lightning flared from the giant's hands as he used flint and steel to kindle his fire. Any moisture evaporated long before hitting the ground. After a spectacular hour-long airborne pyrotechnic display, Max shepherded his flock into their tents.

For most of the scouts, sleep was a long time coming that last night in the mountains. The week was inspected with a microscope. Much had been learned. Most of it filed away to be reviewed at a later time. Before fading off to sleep, Max checked in with The Man in Charge, the great Scoutmaster of all Scouts, giving thanks again for the privilege of working with boys.

The Stage

Steve arrived at the troop meeting early. Max liked punctuality, a trait that had rubbed off on Steve. As senior patrol leader, he needed to make certain that the service patrol had the equipment ready for the meeting. They needed to open the troop's storage room located off the school's lunch room. From it the service patrol had to get out the troop advancement board, the flags, the box of merit badge hooks, and the birch log electric campfire. The custodian had already pulled out a row of bleachers in the gym for the scouts to use. The service patrol needed to set up a long table and chairs for the troop scoutmaster and staff and position the equipment appropriately around the table. Each patrol sat on a bench of the bleachers. The stage was off limits for scouts.

As usual, the service patrol was prompt and had the gym set up for the Tuesday night scout meeting on time. Steve was pleased with the results as he walked outside to meet Max as he parked his car. It turned out that Max was a little late, so Steve returned to the gym to check on the service patrol. They were nowhere to be seen. He checked the restroom but found it empty. Returning to the gym, Steve noticed that the curtain on the stage was moving as if it had just been closed. Still no scouts visible. Then Steve realized that the scouts were on the stage, and that if Max caught them there, trouble was certain to follow.

Steve climbed the stairs to the stage and fumbled in the dark, groping for the light panel so he could illuminate the stage and catch the scouts in the act. Just as he flipped on the light switch, he told the scouts to clear off the stage. They knew it was off limits. As he finished giving his instructions to the errant scouts, Steve heard Max's voice on the other side of the curtain and realized that he had not been in time to keep the service patrol from getting into trouble.

"All of you scouts get out here, now," bellowed Max. "You know you're not supposed to be on the stage."

With a sigh, Steve flipped off the lights and was the last scout to descend the stairs, wondering as he walked what Max was going to say to the service patrol. Steve had tried to save their bacon. He felt badly for them, but perhaps now was a good time for them to learn how to meet Max's expectations.

"I want all of you scouts to go home. If you can follow directions next week, you are welcome to return. Now git! You too, senior patrol leader. Of all people, you should know not to be playing on the stage."

"But Max, I was just . . ." began Steve in explanation.

"You too. Come back next week and try it again," Max said, cutting off Steve's protest. "You should be setting a better example."

Incredulously, Steve headed out the door, angry at the unfairness of Max's position.

"I'll show him," Steve said petulantly to himself. "I'm never coming back to this troop. He can get a new senior patrol leader."

Along the highway, it was three miles home for Steve. Instead, he followed the railroad tracks, which crossed his family's property line after passing through a swamp thick with cedar trees, bullfrogs, and mosquitoes. The shortcut saved him a mile but subjected him to the ravages of a reinforced regiment of airborne aggravation. Steve decided it was worth the price he had to pay. Besides, he was afraid someone would offer him a ride if he hiked along the road and he only wanted solitude in which to cultivate his anger.

As he followed the tracks into the swamp, Steve reflected on the unfairness of Max's decision. He hadn't even asked what Steve was doing on the stage. Max assumed that Steve was part of the problem when in reality Steve was trying to help manage the troop. He was just doing his job.

Plodding along the tracks, head down as he concentrated his efforts in stepping on the ties, Steve became aware of the hundreds of fireflies visible in his peripheral vision. Looking up, he was dazzled by their errant flickering flight. As he watched a bioluminescent beetle floating above a willow, it stopped before settling on a branch where it continued to flash its signal. Another lightning bug approached the one resting on the willow. Their lights seemed to flash in response to each other, signalling a mutual attraction. Steve knew that in some species of fireflies, the female imitated the mating signal of another species so that when a male approached too closely, the female could dine on the fooled insect. Most often, though, the lights were a means of attracting a mate.

Steve realized that, like an unsuspecting beetle responding to an inappropriate stimulus, people could also make mistakes. To Steve, the mistake Max had made seemed monumental. He had been sent home unjustly. But the world wouldn't end because of Max's single error. Steve knew that he had been correct in getting the scouts off from the stage. Instead of wallowing in self-pity like a hog happily rolling in the mud, Steve decided to put the night behind him. Next week he would return to the scouts, resuming his responsibilities as senior patrol leader and setting a better example for the troop.

Whistling as he did so, Steve hopped up on the right hand rail, balancing as he shuffled along and feeling good about his decision to stay in scouts. Steve reached the bank at the edge of his property line and ran up it into his backyard.

"I'm home early," Steve announced to his mom while bursting through the back door. After explaining to her what had happened that prompted his early return, his mom asked Steve if he had learned anything from the incident.

"I guess it's important to gather as much information as possible before making a decision," noted Steve thoughtfully, gazing into the distance, his eyes circling as he reflected. Steve thought about how much hurt he felt when Max had sent him home. "I don't think Max knows how much he hurt me tonight.

97

We need to be gentle with each other as we interact," he added. "It is too easy to unintentionally hurt someone's feelings."

"Try to remember this night, Steve, if you ever get to be a scoutmaster," counseled his mom as she gave him a hug.

Brian's Song

At first the blindfolds had seemed like a good idea. Steve had lost track of time. It seemed like he had been blundering around for hours, unable to either see or talk. His legs told him that he had blindly stumbled into every blackberry bush in the north woods, while heading generally uphill. All of his energy, though, was focused on listening for the sound he had been following for the last hour, certain that he was the only scout left in the troop who was still submitting to the sightless discomfort of blindfolds.

The scouts had started the hike using neckerchiefs for blindfolds. At first all of the scouts held hands as they stumbled over unseen ground, trying desperately to communicate nonverbally, since Max had told them to remain silent until otherwise instructed. Steve had found that he could help the scout behind him climb over a low obstacle by raising their joined hands high over his head. Pulling down on his partner meant that something was endangering their heads. Steve had learned the code from the scout in front of him.

After what seemed like an hour of dodging trees and bushes, Max had broken physical contact between the scouts by giving each of them the end of a stick, grasped desperately at each end by a scout: the serpentine line of scouts connected by wood. Loss of physical contact was extremely uncomfortable for Steve. It seemed like the tenuous line of communication between the scouts ahead and behind him was effectively diminished: a cryptic code of communication had become more difficult to decipher. Movement was very slow as each obstacle was encountered and overcome, and the message of travel passed on to the next scout.

Adding to the discomfort of restricted travel was a nagging thirst. Steve last had a drink early that afternoon before leaving with the rest of the troop on a confidence course arranged by Max. He was certain it was near sunset and the heat and humidity of the northern woods was taking a toll.

For the first time, Steve noticed a sound ahead of him, which seemed like rocks being shaken in a can. Every thirty seconds the can was rattled and the sound was always directly in front of Steve as he struggled with his sticks and nearby scouts. After listening to the can rattle for perhaps five minutes, Steve was startled when he stumbled onto a backwoods road. Ominously, the line stopped and all was quiet. The stick from each hand was removed and a finger pressed gently to Steve's lips, reminding him of the continued need for silence. After five minutes or so, the can was again rattled and Steve strained hard, listening for an indication of what was expected of him. Then the can sound began to move away from him. It dawned on him that he was expected to follow the sound of the can.

Carefully sliding his feet along the ground, Steve slowly followed the sound of the retreating can. Panic nibbled at the edges of his mind. He could hear the sound of the breeze gently rustling the leaves of nearby trees. Farther away he thought he heard the sound of a stream, reminding him again that he was really thirsty. Then Steve focused on a sound that he recognized as the muffled sound of feet nearby. Apparently other scouts were timidly following the rattling sound of rocks in a can as they silently shuffled after their scoutmaster.

The strain of listening so intently, while expecting, at any moment to fall into a gaping chasm was becoming unbearable. At that point, Steve heard another rattling can that seemed to be close to the original can. Their sounds were distinctive but confusing. Which was Steve expected to follow? He tried to concentrate on the first can sound but soon was unable to distinguish one from the other. When the sounds of the cans diverged, Steve stopped in confusion. Someone bumped into him and muttered something unintelligible. Steve quickly decided to follow one of the receding sounds.

He was surprised as his feet left the safety of the road he had been carefully following, and Steve knew he had made a mistake but also that it was too late to retreat. With added caution Steve continued following the nearby rattling sound. As he finally decided that he would survive this latest challenge, Steve stumbled into knee-deep water. His feet sank ankle-deep in ooze on the bottom, which slowed down his progress significantly. Still the rattling sound persisted, though it no longer seemed to be moving. Steve had no choice but to continue on, each step difficult, not knowing if the next would take him into water over his head. He could hear water sloshing and the sound of someone nearby was surprisingly comforting. As Steve approached the rattling can, the water diminished in depth and a hand reached out to help him climb out of the water.

Quietly Max told him to remove his blindfold. In front of him were most of the troop members, blindfolds removed and smiles on their faces. Behind him was a beaver pond inhabited now by two struggling scouts who slogged towards the sound emanating from the can in Max's hand. When the final wayward scouts reached the bank and were helped up, Max invited the scouts in the troop to sit in a circle near the beaver pond.

"Well, fellas, what did you learn?" questioned Max. "Think about it a minute before you answer."

Steve looked at the scratches criss-crossing his legs. He thought of the fear he had experienced as he tried to make sense out of an unreal situation. Steve was especially proud of the way the scouts helped each other overcome obstacles. He remembered the confusion of the difficult can sounds and how he had chosen the can that led him through the beaver pond. He reflected on the feelings he had while in the pond, knowing that he should have followed the other can, but secure in the knowledge that someone else was in the pond with him and he was not alone.

"Teamwork," offered John. "We have to depend on each other."

"Trust," suggested Roy, as he looked at his battered legs. "Max, I thought you were nuts for a while. Then I realized you wouldn't do anything to endanger us, so it got easier for me to follow blindly."

"I agree with them," concluded Gary thoughtfully. "I also had to deal with a lot of fear. It is really difficult to travel without being able to see. I have a great deal of respect for blind people. I wanted to quit."

"You know," began Steve, "I had a really difficult time with the cans. It took me some time to get comfortable following sounds. But when you added a second can, I didn't know what to do. Why'd you do that anyway?"

Max remained silent. He fished his pipe out of a side pocket and knocked it against his boot. After charging the pipe's bowl with cherry-flavored tobacco, Max jammed his pipe in the corner of his mouth. Lighting it with his old wartime Zippo, Max puffed away, the cloud of smoke hiding his face, but not the twinkle in his eyes.

"Why do you think?" he finally responded.

Steve looked around the circle of scouts, looking for assistance. no one responded to his silent plea for help. *Max shouldn't answer a question with a question,* he thought. *It's not fair.* He looked at his hands, dirtied from holding the sticks, searching for an answer in the grime. His boots were muddy, he noticed. His soggy socks held up only by the garters around his upper calf. No answer there either. He thought of his feelings when he first heard the can and later when he realized that he was expected to follow its sound. He looked to the west where the rays from the setting sun broke through the clouds, casting long shafts of light earthward.

"It was our conscience that we were following, wasn't it, Max?" offered Steve as realization lit his mind like the setting sun. "We need to learn to follow the still small voice within that tells us what is right! If we don't, we sometimes get into trouble."

"You guys are sharp," noted Max. "Get a drink upstream from the beaver pond, and let's head out."

"Head out?" said Steve, incredulously. "What about dinner?"

"Dinner? What dinner?" replied Max, his eyes twinkling mischievously.

To Steve, the remainder of the hike seemed endless, worse than any that Pierre had led them on so many years before. At least then they had something to eat before they left. Steve couldn't remember when he had last eaten. His stomach thought his throat had been cut. Through the long, long night, they hiked, detouring around sensed but scarcely seen obstacles, always heading west. The stars came out and wheeled across the sky, following their ancient course. Steve was interested to note how Ursa Major, the Big Dipper, pivoted around the sky, looking different upside down and how only Polaris, the North Star remained constant in position.

Younger scouts became weary and older scouts offered encouragement before finally helping them struggle along the barely discerned trail. Complaints of hunger, thirst, and sore feet finally diminished as legs and feet became numb and minds switched to neutral. Through it all, Max erectly hiked along, offering encouragement as needed, a mountain of energy: the only reason Steve kept going. *If Max can do this, so can I*, he thoughtfully counseled himself.

By sunrise, the scouts had hiked ten miles. They were bleary-eyed, thinking they were starving and on the verge of dehydration. With unfeeling feet, they stumbled into a hollow where two crystalline streams merged in a swirl of sound, collapsing in untidy heaps when Max called a halt. Mysteriously their sleeping bags were already there. Steve staggered to the stream's edge where he bent over and cupped his hands to drink greedily from the cold water. Returning to the sleeping bags, Steve found one that looked vaguely like his, spread it out, collapsed on it without removing even his boots, and was instantly asleep.

After Max determined that everyone was accounted for

and sleeping soundly, he, too, rolled out his sleeping bag, falling into a deep sleep the instant his head stopped moving, ignoring the whine and bite of buzzing mosquitoes.

The heat of the sun awakened everyone at mid-day. Because they hadn't eaten since the previous day, everyone was ravenous. Supper, breakfast, and lunch consisted of two oranges per scout. After gorging themselves on the hearty meal, the scouts peeled off their boots and socks, dangling their feet in the cold stream, before tending to their battered toes and heels. Max helped lance and bandage blisters on most feet, with the notable exception of his own. Max didn't get blisters.

For the rest of the day, each patrol carefully peeled and cut up carrots, onions, and peppers, which were added to browned meat in a huge pot. As the stew bubbled away on banked fires, flour was added to thicken the stew. A handful of seasoning was added for flavor. A half-hour before dinnertime, each patrol made dumplings that were cooked on top of the stew, expanding with the heat to cover the interior of the pot. The tantalizing smells of fresh stew simmering reminded Steve that it had been a long time since he had last eaten anything.

Finally Max decided that the patrols could eat. Each scout savored his portion of stew while keeping a careful eye on the other scouts in the patrol, making certain that each serving was of uniform size and that there would be stew left for second helpings. Max ate as much as anyone. After eating more than he thought possible, Steve decided that he wasn't going to die after all, at least not in the foreseeable future.

That night, fatigue, fear, and pain already diminished, the scouts held a two-hour campfire, singing the old songs, performing stale skits, and listening to Max recite the ancient, but well-received poetry of Robert Service. The scouts had come together as a troop, more so than at any time in Max's memory. He was proud of his scouts. They had faced a serious challenge, helping each other along the way. They had learned that it was possible to always take one more step, even when privately convinced that further movement was impossible. They had grown up some.

The next morning, after loading their sleeping bags and other equipment on a truck, Max hiked with his scouts for five miles along the road until they came to a place where limestone bluffs stood sentry along the stream bank. Max had arranged for older scouts from other troops to help run his patrols through difficult initiative activities as they continued to learn about teamwork and the pride of accomplishing difficult tasks.

At various times, each patrol had to cross a rope bridge that was strung across the stream high up in some tree trunks. A second challenge was to escape from a prisoner-of-war camp over a simulated four-foot high electric fence. Another obstacle was to travel across a simulated mine field, using three-inch square blocks to step on for safety. Each patrol had one fewer block than scouts in the patrol. A fourth problem was figuring out a way to get a stack of oranges out from a thirty-foot circle under a tree without touching the ground inside the circle. Success at this obstacle was important since the oranges were lunch for the scouts. Their final venture was to rappel down a fifty-foot limestone bluff. All of these activities had to be done in silence.

At the conclusion of the day, Max and his troop hiked for another three miles, reaching a meadow hidden in a hollow away from the road as the shadows lengthened with the setting sun.

While Steve's patrol was preparing tin-foil dinners, Max brought two guests to the patrol area.

"This is Brian," said Max. "And this is his father. They will have dinner with you and stay for your patrol campfire."

Without meaning to, Steve stared at Brian. He seemed to be about fourteen years old.

"Hi," said Steve, uncomfortably as he realized that he had been staring. "Welcome to the Eagle Patrol."

Brian's arms and legs were bony, the thickness of a hatchet handle. His head, though normal-sized for a boy his age, seemed incongruously larger than his wasted body. He was carried by his father, who tenderly laid Brian down near the fire's warmth but out of the way.

"I'll be right back," he said, looking at his son, but probably talking to everyone.

When he returned, Brian's father carried a cushion from a lounge chair, which he placed on the ground near Brian. Then, placing one hand under Brian's knees and the other behind his back, his dad carefully lifted Brian from the ground before setting him gently on the cushion.

"Thanks for letting us join your patrol," said Brian's dad, pointing to Brian. "He doesn't get a chance to do much scouting."

Dinner was a quiet affair. All of the scouts seemed wrapped up in private thoughts, though in reality, they were not yet comfortable with Brian.

Later, around the campfire, the scouts began to open up. They talked about how tiring the hike was. None of them had ever hiked all night before. Blisters were a common experience, as all scouts grumbled about having them. Hunger was another pressing issue that was felt by everyone. Through the litany of complaints, Brian offered no comments, his wasted body a caricature in the firelight.

Steve began to focus on the things they had learned. He talked about teamwork and trust, compassion, problem-solving, communication, and finally about his own fear as he stood at the edge of the limestone bluff, willing his legs to move as he struggled against the notion of leaning backwards into the rope to begin the descent. He shared with them how his legs quivered up and down in an uncontrollable spasm of fear, which he was finally able to overcome. More than the fear, though, was the pride he felt when he reached the bottom of the bluff and realized what he had done. The smile on his face had been continent-wide and he had stepped away from the bluff with a lengthened stride.

Finally, as the flames sputtered and died, leaving only a bed of glowing coals, Brian spoke for the first time. "You know,

I've never had a blister on my foot," and he smiled as he said it. "I can't remember ever being hungry. I certainly never went a day without eating," he said, leaning on an emaciated elbow, looking every bit like a concentration camp survivor. "But I have an experience each day that you will never have," Brian said, as he looked down at his interlocked fingers. He studied them for a long time. When he finally look up again, tears had overflowed his eyes and cascaded down his cheeks. "Everything I do," he said. "I get to do in my father's arms."

In the silence that followed, Steve's eyes and heart turned heavenward, towards *The Man in Charge*. Remembering the parts of the scout oath and law that talked about reverence and duty to God, Steve vowed to try to live so that he was worthy to do everything in his Father's arms.

Sea Gulls

The silent gulls were soaring on the wind above the water near the edge of the lake, brilliant white against the cyanean sky. Wings held steady and facing into the breeze, the gulls controlled their position over the water with delicate movements of feathers as they changed the angle and surface area of their wings. Graceful kites on invisible strings, the gulls effortlessly rode the gentle morning zephyrs on coal-tipped wings. Side-to-side movements of their heads allowed their gimlet ebony eyes to survey the surface below, looking for dead fish or other flotsam on which to dine.

"Breakfast Flock," thought Max, seeing in his mind's eye the life of his friend, Jonathan Livingston Seagull, an Eagle scout of gulls.

One gull, grayer than the others, suddenly swooped down to the beach, landed briefly, and delicately snatched a morsel of food in her curved yellow beak, before flapping her wings furiously to gain both altitude and solitude. Her maneuver was noted by other gulls in the flock, who, seeing the young gull with her tasty tidbit, immediately gave chase. Max watched the birds near the lake by his home, fascinated by the gulls cartwheeling across the sky, now like feathered fireworks. The gull with the morsel seemed to be fleeing for her very life, dodging, turning, and twisting through the air: a dervish of whirling wings. Frenetically, she flashed through tree tops, turning violently to avoid imminent wooden collisions before frantically beating her wings in a vertical power climb. The rest of the gulls in the flock matched her turn for turn as she soared high in the air before descending in a shrieking dive, attempting to evade her tormentors. Young and strong, this breakfast gull flew with confidence, maintaining a lead on the other gulls, though not able to pull away.

She flew with grace and finesse but lacked the experience of the flock. Together, they began to turn inside her arcs, shortening the distance they had to fly to catch her, drawing closer to the inevitable moment when she became too tired for evasive actions. Finally, when it became apparent that the energy expended while evading the flock would not be replaced by the piece of bread clutched desperately in her mouth, the young gull dropped her bakery bit of breakfast. It tumbled through the air and landed some distance down the beach from where Max was standing. Incredibly, the Breakfast Flock immediately gave up the chase and returned to the open water where they resumed navigating into the wind, heads rotating on feathered necks, eyes scanning anew. None of the gulls even noticed the fallen feast. None descended to claim the relinquished prize. The young gull rejoined the flock as they continued riding the morning breeze.

Throughout the day Max reflected upon his morning's experience of watching the gulls at the lake. Why had the flock given up when the young gull dropped the hunk of bread? Why did no gull attempt to retrieve the fallen morsel? That evening at scout meeting, during his scoutmaster's minute, Max shared his observations with his troop. He told them of the grace and courage of the gallant young gull and of her attempts to flee from the rest of the flock so that she could dine in peace. And of the harassment from the rest of the flock until she finally succumbed to the overbearing pressure, dropping the bread in her exhaustion before flapping away to resume her position with the remainder of the flock.

"Scouts are sometimes like the young gull," he told them. "By gathering up the bit of bread, the young gull became different from the rest of the flock. Sometimes flocks won't let gulls be different. These gulls chased the distinguished gull until she dropped the bread, losing what she had that made her different. When the gray gull was more like the rest of the

109

flock, the others stopped chasing her.

"People are sometimes like that," continued Max, as he tried to make sense of what he had seen. "A square person in a round society will probably have difficulty similar to the gray gull. Like the gulls, people will carefully chip away at the corners of her character until she becomes smooth and spherical.

"A scout who wears a full uniform, shows a lot of scout spirit, and lives by the Scout Oath and Law, will be different from other people. Society may tease the scout because of the good things for which he stands rather than respect him for his courage to be different. They may harass him, chasing him through life, trying to make him feel different *bad* rather than different *unique*.

"It is often easier to drop the bread to stop the pursuit than it is to continue dodging the flock. It is important for you to know that the strength needed to be different is tremendous. But the rewards reaped by being a square scout are worth the sometimes painful price exacted by a round society. Hold on to the bread, scouts. Continue to dodge. Remember that you are *always* a scout, not just when in uniform and that the spirit of Baden-Powell is the strength of scouting."

The lessons taught by Max to scouts have spanned generations. His influence continues on, like ripples in the sea of life, sent forever outward by the splash made by a rock of a scouter. Seen from a lofty perspective, his waves will wash upon unseen shores and affect the lives of people Max will never meet.

After thirty-three years, Max retired as scoutmaster of Troop 35. During that time, he served as scoutmaster to three generations of scouts. At a court of honor recognizing the achievements of a young scout in his troop, near the end of his tenure as scoutmaster, Max was surprised to note the presence of both the father and grandfather of his new Tenderfoot scout. Both had been scouts in Max's troop. They were three of about 850 scouts who had been members of the troop when Max was scoutmaster, and whose ranks formed a long green line that marched to the drumbeat of the spirit of scouting from the campfires of the distant past to the ideas of the future, carrying with them a bit of the love of scouting given to them by a selfless scoutmaster to cherish in a quiet corner of their hearts when they reflected on the forces that had shaped their lives. Each of them would quietly, but with great pride, grasp the little finger of their right hand with their thumb in a scout sign, and, bringing their hand crisply to their forehead, render a scout salute in honor of their friend and scoutmaster, John A. Maxbauer, Jr.

Afterword

As a young scout in Traverse City, Michigan, I was fortunate in having John A. Maxbauer, Jr. as my scoutmaster. From him I learned a love of the outdoors, invaluable leadership skills, an understanding of a boy's sense of humor, and the importance of honor. In him I saw a man who lived the Scout Oath and Law and the Outdoor Code. With him I camped, hiked, advanced, canoed, and shed a few tears. To him and the Boy Scouts of America, I owe an incalculable debt, one that I have spent years repaying. In 1991, our scout troop was without a permanent home. We decided to build a log cabin for our scouting family. In November of 1993, we dedicated the John A. Maxbauer, Jr. Scout Lodge as the permanent home of Troop 999. In February of 1996, in the building that bears his name, John Maxbauer presented the Eagle Award to Scott W. Chapman, the second of my sons to receive this award.

Throughout the story I referred to my scoutmaster as Max, a name I never used as a boy or as an adult when thinking of him. His good wife, Lillian, was a second mother to me. A few years ago, my son and I were visiting the Maxbauers. Lil "adopted" Scott as if he was her own son, something I saw her do numerous times when I was a youth. Watching them visit in her kitchen carried me back to the days and evenings I spent as a youth in the kitchen of their big house. The warmth and acceptance I felt as a boy were shared with my son. He felt a part of the Maxbauer family.

Throughout the book Pierre appears as himself. With fond memories do I remember the Legends of Pierre. Sadly I have not seen him in over twenty-five years. Joe, Ham, and Lenny were probably my closest friends in scouting. They appear throughout the story, with each having an assumed name. Today Joe is a schoolteacher in our hometown where Ham treats animals as a veterinarian. Lenny retired following a distinguished career as an Armor Officer in the U.S. Army. I also owe a debt to Jim, Gary, Tom, Mike, and all of the other scouts of Troop 35. With them and from them, I learned much. My younger brother, Dave, also an Eagle Scout, has imparted many lessons to me.

I have taken the liberty of combining the characters and mannerisms of several scouts in the retelling of some of their stories. For convenience some of my experiences have been combined. Anyone who has served as a scout leader will recognize these boys as having been in their troop at one time or another. Hopefully we can all identify with these boys and honor the diversity among them.

Among the scouts with whom I currently serve, I would like to recognize and thank the members of the Rocking Chair Patrol. Blair and Chet are sorely missed. Ken is needed. Andy is The Bear. He leads our rolling circus on our many adventures throughout the West. With him we can always plan on having a hot time. Hopefully the West will, in time, recover from our visits. Dave, Ted, two Steves, John, and the two Dons rock along beside me. Together we will someday have our own wing in a retirement center where we will probably be kept in isolation as we tell stories around an imaginary campfire. A few of the stories will undoubtedly be true.

Lyn is my wife and she used to be an Eagle. She has steadfastly supported our scouting program and been there when we needed her. With my sons, John and Scott, I have attended a National Jamboree, a Russian International Jamboree and the National Order of the Arrow Conference. Together we have logged many nights of camping and hiked for miles down many trails. The four of us completed a fifty-mile hike in seventeen hours as part of a troop project. We crossed the finish line together. Analee has been there always. While not a scout, she has learned scouting skills and practiced them with Outward

Bound in Oregon. Todd is about to become a Boy Scout. Hopefully he will follow the trails blazed by his older brothers.

The Philmont Scout Ranch in Cimarron, New Mexico, has played a significant part in my life and the experiences of my family. I am a lifetime member of the Philmont Staff Association. Both Lyn and I completed Wood Badge Training at Philmont while hiking its secluded trails. John and Scott have attended the National Junior Leader Instructor Training Course at the Rocky Mountain Scout Camp where John also served on staff. They have both participated in the Trail Building program sponsored by the Order of the Arrow. I would like to express my appreciation to all of the current and past staff members at Philmont for providing a supportive, inviting atmosphere to all who visit there. In the name of John Maxbauer, a portion of the proceeds of each book sold will be donated to the Philmont Staff Association to continue their fine work. Jim and Valerie at the Cimarron Art Gallery and Martin and Linda at the Cimarron Inn have been most delightful in our yearly trips to New Mexico. We feel at home while with them and appreciate their constant hospitality.

Marilyn Schuldt Chapman is deceased. She died when our children were two, four, and seven years old. In our life together, she positively affected the lives of our children and many others in the neighborhood. She would be proud of her children. Finally I would like to thank Randy, Art, Corey, Hooker, Doug, my partner in climb, Doc, and Oz for a lifetime of friendship. They have been rock steady in their support. Debbie, Dorie, Cheree, and Sarah have been the fragrance of the bouquet of Grandview learning. I would pick flowers with them anywhere.

—The Author

2565973

Made in the USA